"Can you  he barke

"I'm a trained secretary," Delfi answered tartly. "Why?"

"Because I might have a use for your services, that's why!" he slammed back at her.

"My secretarial services?" Delfi, who'd been caught napping once before, remained belligerent.

The look of dislike he threw at her would have curdled milk. He had no need to add that he liked his women to have pleasing personalities—it was obvious he found Delfi difficult.

"Forgive me for being blunt," he replied icily, looking anything but sorry, "but even should I fancy you—" a fair hint there that margarine would turn to butter before that happened "—I've never paid for those kind of services, nor do I intend to start!"

Jessica Steele first tried her hand at writing romance novels at her husband's encouragement two years after they were married. She fondly remembers the day her first novel was accepted for publication. ''Peter mopped me up, and neither of us cooked that night,'' she recalls. ''We went out to dinner.'' She and her husband live in a hundred-year-old cottage in Worcestershire, and they've traveled to many fascinating places—including China, Japan, Mexico and Denmark—that make wonderful settings for her books.

Books by Jessica Steele

Don't miss any of our special offers. Write to us at the following address for information on our newest releases.

Harlequin Reader Service
P.O. Box 1397, Buffalo, NY 14240
Canadian address: P.O. Box 603,
Fort Erie, Ont. L2A 5X3

RUNAWAY FROM LOVE
Jessica Steele

Harlequin Books

TORONTO • NEW YORK • LONDON
AMSTERDAM • PARIS • SYDNEY • HAMBURG
STOCKHOLM • ATHENS • TOKYO • MILAN
MADRID • WARSAW • BUDAPEST • AUCKLAND

Original hardcover edition published in 1991
by Mills & Boon Limited

ISBN 0-373-03203-X

Harlequin Romance first edition June 1992

RUNAWAY FROM LOVE

CHAPTER ONE

HER decision, Delfi mused when, keeping her unhappy feelings down, she paused in her packing that Sunday evening, had not been so much a decision she had made after weeks of thinking things over very carefully. Or even, she solemnly reflected, of days of thinking things over very carefully. If the truth be known, it had been more a case of everything snowballing on from that one incident last Monday when she had finally lost her temper with Mr Yardley, her boss—now her ex-boss—and had walked out of her job.

Prior to that she had, of course, known for some time that something, something very drastic, would have to be done if her sister Raina was not to be desperately hurt for a second time. But what that something was had not become clear to Delfi until after things had come to a head at the office last Monday. Usually, she was slow to anger, but, instead of biting her tongue when yet again Mr Yardley had pushed the blame on to her for something which he had left undone, she had found that it proved to be once too often. She had exploded, and followed through by clearing out her desk.

Delfi, her mind elsewhere, took a rest from her packing and went over to the padded chair in her bedroom. She was barely aware of her actions but, in no time, thoughts of Mr Yardley were replaced by other thoughts. And as ever Hugh Renshaw, the man her sister was going to marry, was there in her head.

Her thoughts flew back to how Hugh had come to declare that he loved her and not Raina. She admitted

5

that she was a little confused about how it had all happened, but oh, how she wished that it never had. Surely things would not have been as impossible as they now were if Hugh had never taken her in his arms that time when, her parents out, Raina not yet back from some errand, he had arrived early and found her alone.

Raina was twenty-seven and had been engaged to Hugh for eight months, and had no idea that Delfi, her junior by five years, had grown to love the same man. Delfi had been most careful that no one else should know of it either, but somehow, she had realised only on that fateful day Hugh had arrived and found her the sole occupant of the house, he had known.

'Little Delfi!' he'd exclaimed softly, the way he called her 'little Delfi' thrilling her despite the fact that he at five ten was only two inches taller than she was. She smiled at him, and suddenly he was pulling her into his arms. And she, to her everlasting shame, forgot all about her sister.

She welcomed his lips, his embrace, and returned his kisses mindless of everything as, there in the hall of the home she shared with her parents and her sister, there was no thought in her head for anyone except Hugh.

'Who could resist your provocative, inviting mouth?' Hugh murmured as he briefly pulled back. Then, just before he kissed her again, 'Or who could fail to love you?' he asked.

'You—love me?' she asked, as soon as she had breath left to ask anything, her violet-coloured eyes large, questioning.

'As you love me,' he admitted, and had been about to kiss her again when all at once, to mortifyingly bring Delfi crashing abruptly back to earth, the sound of someone inserting a key in the front door penetrated.

Guiltily they sprang apart. 'Raina!' Delfi choked, horror-struck, pulling away from Hugh, and, absolutely swamped by the sudden and most dreadful feeling of remorse, she pelted up the stairs to her room, too shamed to be able to face her sister.

She stayed in her room and remained there even when fifteen minutes later she heard her sister and future brother-in-law leave the house. She heard Hugh's car start up but could not even go to the window. All she could think of was how Raina had been engaged once before. Of how, four years ago, she had been jilted and how she had taken it so badly that for an age they had feared that she would never get over it.

With her spirits swung so swiftly from the heights to the very depths, Delfi knew then that there was no future for her with Hugh Renshaw. It was clear, by the very fact that he and Raina had gone out for the evening as planned, that Hugh had told Raina nothing of what had so recently taken place in the hall downstairs.

Nor must he. Nor, most definitely, Delfi realised, would she. What happiness could there be for her and Hugh if, as a result of being jilted a second time, her sister had a breakdown that was worse than the time before?

Delfi spent a sleepless night hoping and praying that Hugh had said nothing of their love for each other to her sister. With fear in her heart she went down to breakfast the next morning and felt so mixed up then that she didn't know whether to laugh or cry when Raina, as sweet as ever she was, greeted her with a friendly, cheerful and even teasing, 'Will this be the day that sneaky Yardley gets your notice?'

Delfi managed a grin. 'Did I tell you what he did yesterday?' she tried for normality, and later went to her office with Mr Yardley and his sneaky ways the least of her worries.

During the next few days she came to the resolution that, while her feelings for Hugh had not changed, she and Hugh were going to have to pretend that those shared weak moments between them had never happened.

The only problem there, she found, was that Hugh was not of the same mind. For while Delfi was putting everything she had into being strong, Hugh constantly tried to undermine her strength by seeking to get her alone at every opportunity. At those instances she strove hard, in the short space of time available, to try and get through to him that they could not hurt Raina. But, to undermine what remaining strength she had still further, he would render her words as nothing—by taking her in his arms.

Matters had gone on like that for a month with Delfi starting to panic that if she didn't soon do something— though without knowing what she could do—then Raina was bound to guess. Either that or Hugh—for all he made an outward show of being as much in love with Raina as ever—might crack if he was feeling the strain anywhere as near as much as Delfi, and might end his engagement. Delfi panicked some more at that thought. Whatever happened, he must not do that.

Things reached a peak though when, for the first time ever, Hugh rang her at her place of work and suggested that she met him away from her home that evening. Delfi knew that Raina had not arranged to see him that night, but she couldn't, just couldn't, go behind her sister's back in such a blatant fashion.

'I can't,' Delfi heard her own voice refuse, and started to panic again in case he insisted and made her weak to the point of blatant treachery—she had honestly done her best to avoid being left alone with him on those other occasions. It was then that Delfi, who could not remember the last time she had uttered a lie, forced the words out, 'I already have a date for tonight.' With that, and with what little moral fibre she had left, she quietly put the phone down.

When at lunchtime that day one of the other secretaries with whom she was friendly invited her to a party that night, Delfi accepted with alacrity. A party was the last thing she needed just now, but it helped to ease her irritating conscience about her lie—even if the lie was in a good cause.

It was at the party that she met Melvin 'Call me Mel' Dalloway. He was about the same height and build as Hugh but, where Hugh was a fairly confident type of man, Mel Dalloway seemed confident to the point of being brash. And, where Hugh had lived all his life in London, Mel, to hear him talk, had been everywhere. He was, it turned out, at present on leave from his manager's job in an export and import company in Thailand.

'Do you get home to England often?' Delfi, since she'd accepted the invitation to the party, did her best to be sociable with a fellow guest.

'About a couple of times a year,' he replied, propping himself up against a wall with one hand while leaning over her to explain, 'There's a worldwide exhibition coming up in Bangkok shortly,' adding importantly, 'The firm have called me back for a briefing.' He then went on at some length about his work, and then asked, 'What sort of work do you do?'

'Secretarial,' Delfi replied.

'With looks like that!' he exclaimed, eyeing her silver-blonde hair, clear complexion and violet eyes in some disbelief. 'You're kidding!' and when Delfi shook her head, 'I took you for a photographic model, at least.' From there he went on to tell her that, if ever she felt

the need for a more exciting time of it than living out
her secretarial days in a stuffy London office, he could
always make use of her skills.

Delfi took that with a pinch of salt, but found him
harmless enough as he went on to question how she had
got the name Delfi and proceeded to flirt with her mildly
for the rest of the evening.

With her heart given to Hugh, she had no particular
interest in Mel Dalloway, but he was easy to talk to, and
she had no objection to his offer of seeing her home.
She had every objection, though, when he seemed to
think that driving her back to her home entitled him to
more than a peck on her cheek.

'Some girls do,' she told him shortly, pushing him
firmly away, 'I *don't*!'

'No!' he exclaimed in amazement. 'I can't have such
rotten luck!' And when he could see that he did indeed
have such rotten luck, 'Out of all the women at that
party, trust me to pick the only bloody virgin.' Suddenly
then, though, he laughed, and Delfi discovered at that
point that she quite liked him. So much so that when,
hearing her laugh too, he suddenly said, 'I'm here until
Monday morning—fancy a date tomorrow?' she found
herself agreeing.

From then she saw Mel Dalloway every evening of his
stay. Given that his one aim in life seemed to be to get
her to go to bed with him, otherwise he was easy to get
along with, and to some degree while she was out with
him she thought less frequently of Hugh Renshaw.

She had still not been able to think what she was going
to do about Hugh, however, when, seated with Mel
outside her home on Sunday evening, Hugh, with Raina
beside him, pulled up in front of them.

'Would you like to come in?' Delfi turned her attention swiftly back to Mel.

'I'd better get back to my hotel and see about getting my things packed—I'm off in the morning,' he reminded her.

'So you are.' Delfi smiled, but couldn't resist a quick look to the car in front. Hugh was standing by his car looking straight at them, and even in the dark of that late October evening she knew that he could see well enough to make out that it was her. 'I shall miss you,' she turned again to tell Mel, an anxious kind of note there in her voice.

'You sound as though you really mean that!' Mel exclaimed, clearly pleased, and, never one to miss an opportunity, his arm came along the back of her seat and he leant over and made a thorough job of kissing her. 'Well!' he exclaimed when eventually he pulled back. 'I do believe you've been holding out on me, Miss Washington.'

Delfi felt slightly ashamed of herself, knowing full well that she had used him—perhaps hoping to show Hugh that she did not really care for him after all.

'Er—one kiss doesn't make a—a promise,' she tried to tell Mel lightly, and had never felt so uncomfortable in her life.

'You're saying you're not coming back to my hotel with me?' he guessed.

'I—like you, but—er—I have to go in,' Delfi replied, sorely wishing that she was in her room tucked up in bed and that the rest of the world would go away.

But life wasn't that simple, and her response to Mel's kiss together with her words seemed to have given him food for some thought. For, after a very few moments, he was asking, and he sounded quite serious, 'Like me enough to come to Bangkok to work for me?'

'Work for you?' Delfi replied, starting to feel a little better about using Mel the way she had; plainly he was the sort who never let an opportunity pass. 'What sort of work?' she queried, her tone lightly scoffing.

'Secretarial—straight up,' he replied instantly, and went on to stress that, what with the exhibition he'd told her about starting soon and the orders he expected to get from it, a secretary who could type perfect English would be invaluable to him in the coming months.

'You sound serious,' Delfi murmured, still not one hundred per cent convinced.

'Just hop on a jumbo,' he said grandly, and when Delfi just had to laugh, 'I mean it,' he stressed, sounding slightly peeved that she did not seem to be taking him seriously. 'Look, here's my business card,' he said, fishing inside his jacket pocket and handing it to her. 'Think about it,' he urged, and leaning forward to kiss her again he breathed in her ear, 'Give me a ring from Bangkok airport.'

'I'll—er—think about it, as you say,' Delfi answered, knowing that she wouldn't as she searched for the door-handle. She had the car door open with nothing remaining to be said except to wish him happy landings.

'I really *do* mean it, Delfi,' he insisted before she could wish him anything. 'I'll be waiting for your call.'

Delfi was by then half persuaded that he really did mean it. But, as she stepped on to the short drive of her home and he drove away, so Mel Dalloway went completely from her mind. For leaving the house, proving that this evening he hadn't stayed for his usual cup of coffee, was Hugh.

He was coming straight towards her, but any idea Delfi might have nursed that she might have shown Hugh that she didn't care so much for him after all vanished when, reaching her, he demanded, 'How could you?' and while she stood silent, guilty, and ashamed, 'How could you let another man kiss you when you're in love with me?'

And while she started to shrivel up inside, 'Did you do it deliberately to torture me, to make me jealous?' he angrily wanted to know, and shot out his hands as though intending to take a hold of her.

But Delfi had had more than enough. Without a word she fleet-footedly stepped round to where her mother's car was parked, and, evading his arms, she went racing indoors. Once she had the door closed, however, she realised that she couldn't charge up to her bedroom and the solitude it provided without first observing the courtesy of popping her head round the sitting-room door.

'I'm back,' she said lightly to her parents, who were in the middle of watching a film on television.

'So Raina said,' her father observed. 'What's the matter with this one that you couldn't bring him in?' he went on to tease.

'He has a plane to catch,' she said lightly, and with a smile to her sister who was seated in one of the chairs in the room with a warm drink, 'I'm off to bed,' she said generally.

It took her a long time to get to sleep that night. Hugh was in her mind a lot of the time and how, without meaning to, it seemed that all she had succeeded in doing when she'd allowed Mel to kiss her was to make Hugh jealous.

Delfi felt weary as she got out of bed the next morning. And, weary and scratchy-tempered and still searching to know what the dickens she could do, she went to her place of work. Within three hours of leaving her home, she was back there again—Mr Yardley had chosen the wrong morning to lyingly declare, in her hearing, 'It's that secretary of mine, I told her most particularly to let you have it by five o'clock last Friday.' Delfi, most particularly, let him have her instant notice, and walked out.

Her mother was out at a coffee morning when she arrived home. Delfi went upstairs to her room. Her initial fury with Mr Yardley had abated by then, but she in no way regretted doing what she had. She changed into some casual clothes, reflecting that it had only been a matter of time anyway before she handed in her notice and left to find an employer she could respect.

With some vague idea of making herself a cup of coffee, she was just about to leave her room when, on a small antique writing-table, she spotted the business card she had dropped there last night.

Suddenly, as she went over to the table and picked up Mel Dalloway's business card, she not only realised that if she needed another employer she did not need to look very far, but something else as well. Startlingly, then, everything began to fall into place.

All thought of having a cup of coffee went from her mind when in a shaken sort of way she went and sat on the edge of her bed—and thought everything through.

'I really *do* mean it,' she recalled Mel insisting, when doubts began to nudge—would there be any job for her if she took off for Thailand? 'I'll be waiting for your call,' he'd emphasised. But she had to think positive—this was the answer. She needed a way out—this had to be *it*!

Delfi was still rethinking things through when, half an hour later, with her passport and building society savings book in her bag, she left the house—and made for the nearest travel agent to begin her enquiries.

It would pain her to leave her home and to give up all chance of seeing Hugh, but now that this answer had come to her it was a mystery to her why she hadn't thought of it sooner! If she could work in Bangkok for

Mel Dalloway, say for a year, then surely in that year Hugh might forget her.

Delfi hardened her heart against the hurt that Hugh might so soon forget her, but, as she later made her way to the Thai Embassy to apply for a visa—necessary if she was to stay in Thailand for longer than two weeks, she had been informed—she recalled Hugh being angrily ready to take her to task last night and knew that she couldn't face another, more prolonged scene with him.

Which meant, it suddenly hit her, that she was going to have to keep her plans a closely guarded secret from everyone—until the very last moment! For surely Raina would tell Hugh what was afoot if she knew.

In the week that followed, Delfi, feeling awash with guilt each time one of her parents smiled her way, continued with her plans. It distressed her to be so deceptive, but she was anxious at all costs to avoid a confrontation with Hugh where he might insist that she went nowhere near an airport—and when she might yet be weak enough to give in.

'You seem to be having a spring clean!' Raina declared, coming into her bedroom unannounced one evening, and observing the array of clothing on Delfi's bed.

'You know how it is,' she replied lightly, 'a wardrobe full of clothes and nothing to wear. I—er—thought I'd have a clear-out.'

'When you've done yours, you can come and do mine ' Raina laughed, and Delfi felt then as she looked at her blonde-haired, hazel-eyed sister, unlike her in looks and so dear to her, that no sacrifice was too great for her.

Feeling suddenly choked, Delfi knew that Raina would think she'd gone mad had she walked over to her and given her a hug. 'You're on,' she grinned, as she hid her feelings and silently begged her forgiveness.

Her flight was booked for Monday, and as that day neared Delfi grew certain that she was doing the right thing. A year out of the country, she became more and more convinced, was the only answer. To a certain extent, she felt that she had already cut any link with Hugh. She purposely avoided being anywhere around when he called, and knew, if Raina hadn't told him that she'd left Kenyon Cylinders, that he'd be wasting his time if he rang there again attempting to speak with her. She couldn't see him ringing her home during the day either— not when there was every chance that her mother would answer the phone.

Her home was warm and loving, and because it was so Delfi knew that she could not just drop it out on Sunday that she was leaving in the morning for a year or so—not without some lead-up anyhow. Which was why, throughout that week, whenever the chance arose, she would drop out Mel Dalloway's name. And even on one occasion, when talking about getting another job, she, while flooded with guilt, made a deal about the fact that he had offered her a job in Thailand which might be worth thinking about.

When Sunday finally arrived, Delfi began to feel sick in her stomach about what she had to do. As evening approached and the time when Hugh Renshaw was due to call for Raina drew near, Delfi went upstairs to her room feeling more churned up inside than ever.

A heavy weight of sadness descended as she got out her suitcase and began to load it. She could not summon up so much as a glimmer of excitement about her forthcoming trip when, absently, she took a break in her bedroom chair.

She was brought abruptly out of her reverie when she heard her mother calling, 'Do you want any supper, Delfi?'

Delfi went to the top of the stairs, and looked down at the trim attractive woman who was the best mother anyone could have. 'No, thanks, Mum,' she smiled.

'What are you doing up there all this time?' her mother wanted to know.

'Er—sorting through some clothes,' Delfi replied, and smiled again, and hoped her smile hid that her heart was aching.

'Still?' Her mother headed for the kitchen while Delfi went back to her room with an ever-growing feeling of impending doom.

An hour later she heard Raina and Hugh returning from their date. Delfi stayed where she was. Thirty-seven minutes after that, voices floated up the stairway, and Delfi knew that Raina was going to the door with Hugh to say goodnight.

She heard the front door close, and knew that the moment she had been dreading was here. Before she could leave her room, though, she heard Raina coming up the stairs. Then her bedroom door was being pushed inwards. 'Mother says to tell you...' she began, then saw the large suitcase on her bed. 'What's going on?' she exclaimed in total surprise. 'What are you doing?'

I'm doing what I have to, Delfi thought, but answered, 'I'm going to Thailand. I've a job there.'

'*Since when?*' Raina exclaimed.

'Aren't you excited for me?' Delfi countered. 'I couldn't be more pleased myself.'

'Do Mum and Dad know?' Raina queried, seeming puzzled that she was the last one to know.

'I've kept putting off telling them, and putting it off,' Delfi replied, making for the door. 'I'm leaving in the morning.'

'In the *morning*!' Raina echoed incredulously. But, recovering fast, 'They'll skin you!' she opined and, best friend that she was to Delfi, 'I'd better come with you.'

Her parents did not skin her, but to say that they were shaken when Delfi told them what she had to was an understatement. Astonishment came near to covering their reaction when, regardless that his favourite programme was showing on television, her father switched the set off.

'You're going—*where*?' he questioned sternly, causing Delfi to think that if she'd said she was off to Mars his reaction couldn't have been more severe.

'I told you all about the job I'd been offered.' She struggled to stay as near to the truth as she could.

'Then you'd better tell me again,' he said, for one of the rare times coming the heavy-handed father.

Delfi went through her rehearsed routine of how Mel Dalloway had made her the firm offer of a job, and how, since she was now jobless, she had decided to accept his offer.

'It will be really exciting.' She warmed enthusiastically to her theme. 'There'll be a lot to learn, of course, all about the export and import business. Mel will make straight for the airport to meet me the minute I ring him to tell him I've arrived. He——'

'I think it will be a better idea if you ring him now before you get that far,' her father said firmly and Delfi, with more than a little relief, knew that one of the largest hurdles was over in that her father seemed to be accepting that she would be on that plane in the morning.

'I can't ring him at his office now, it won't be open,' she answered, only then remembering that it must be early morning in Bangkok. 'Thai time is seven hours in front of ours.'

When she eventually got to bed that night, her father, if very reluctantly, had given her his blessing about leaving home. She did not sleep well—she hardly expected to—and was up early the next morning with much to do and there seeming little time before her mother drove her to the airport.

At her father's bidding she attempted to ring Mel Dalloway, but a prettily accented female voice informed her that he was out of the office, and Delfi felt a bit unsure about leaving a message that she was on her way to take up secretarial duties. For all she knew Mel might want that information kept confidential until he'd had time to tell whoever normally dealt with his English correspondence that someone was coming to help who was more familiar with the language.

'You'd better send a cable,' her father commented when she had relayed everything to him.

Delfi held back tears as she hugged and kissed both her father and Raina goodbye. She was still holding down tears when at the airport her mother gave her a special hug and asked, with far more insight than Delfi had realised, 'Did you really put off telling us because you thought we'd be upset?'

'Mum...' Delfi uttered helplessly, and suddenly found it impossible to lie to her.

'You're a good girl,' her mother said softly, and there were tears in her eyes when, giving her a gentle push, 'You'd better go,' she said, smiling, and looking at her Delfi knew then that her mother had a fair idea of how she felt about her sister's fiancé.

'Bye,' she murmured, choked, and went quickly before either of them should break down in tears.

The Thai International flight landed in Bangkok at twenty to eight, Thai time, on Tuesday morning. Delfi had by then been through a whole range of emotions

and, if not feeling any more cheerful than she had, she
was of the view, as she cleared passport control and went
to claim her luggage, that the worst—the parting—was
behind her.

It would be nice to see Mel Dalloway again, she told
herself firmly, as she trundled her trolley-borne case
through the 'Nothing to declare' area and speedily
searched for that one face she was looking for.

She could see no sign of Mel, though, and turned
slowly about searching for a telephone. She felt fairly
certain that he would have received her cable, and wondered if he'd been delayed in traffic.

She was wondering if she should perhaps give him
another ten minutes when suddenly a tall, grim-
expressioned, fair-haired man of about thirty-five came
striding into the arrivals area. I shouldn't like to be the
person he's come to meet, Delfi promptly decided, ar-
rested by the sheer authority emanating from the man
she watched as, topping everyone around by a good six
inches, he took the briefest scan of the area. When,
barely hesitating in his stride, he moved and seemed to
be making in a direct line straight for her, though, Delfi
felt her heart give a definite flip. As he halted, and
planted his long lean length slap bang in front of her,
she felt the least she should do was to stand smartly to
attention.

She did not do that, however, but, hoping she looked
as cool as she was trying to make out, she stared with
solemn violet eyes back at the man's even and good-
looking features.

Her cool very nearly deserted her, though, when he
barked impatiently, 'Adelfia Washington?'

It was on the tip of her tongue to smartly retort, 'Yes,
but your name escapes me.' But one glance at his cold
eyes, which were neither blue nor green but something

in between, was all that was needed for her to know that any such utterances would see him arrogantly turning about and striding off without her.

'You've been sent to meet me?' she enquired instead, and knew that was a mistake too the instant the words were out. Arctic was the look he favoured her with; clearly a man who did nobody's errands, without another word, and as if her large overstuffed suitcase weighed nothing, he hefted it off the trolley and strode off without her anyway.

Hoisting her flight bag over her shoulder, Delfi hurried outside after him where he had a limousine waiting. It hurt her pride intensely that in the absence of Mel Dalloway being there to meet her she had to accept this taciturn man's unsociable assistance. But, by the look of it, it was that or be left high and dry!

Her luggage was in the boot and she was seated in the rear beside him in the chauffeur-driven vehicle when they moved off. It was then that she supposed she should be grateful that, in place of Mel, someone had met her at all. She decided to bring her best manners to the fore.

'You're a friend of Mel's?' she enquired politely, even if privately she was of the opinion that Mel and this aristocratic-looking type were from very different stables.

'No,' the fair-haired man rudely grunted, and Delfi heartily wished that she had saved not only her breath but her best manner too. Having noted that he was English, she had just made up her mind that she was not going to address another single solitary word to the impossible creature when he demanded, 'Where to?' and she realised that, not only was he not a friend of Mel Dalloway, but he didn't even know where his offices were.

It was getting on for nine o'clock by that time. Delfi hoped that most business offices were open by nine, and diving into her flight bag she extracted Mel Dalloway's business card and wordlessly handed it, unspeaking, to her unspeakable companion.

She was staring out of the window when he told the driver where to make for, and spent the next forty-five minutes intent on pretending he wasn't there.

Bangkok was noisy, bustling and busy, she observed, and, in common with the few capital cities she'd visited, its traffic was a nightmare. She would swear that the last snarl-up they had been caught up in had seen nothing moving at all for at least ten minutes. Traffic-lights too, in this city where motorbikes abounded, seemed to take an inordinately long time to change. Her thoughts wandered to the man seated next to her and she couldn't help wondering why, when he obviously resented the chore of having to meet her, he had agreed to do so. Why...?

Hastily she dragged her thoughts away from him; soon, surely, she would arrive at Mel's offices. With luck, this would be the one and only time she need have anything to do with his most unwilling envoy.

They had just cleared another ten-minute-long traffic hold-up and Delfi was on the point of wondering if she would ever get to Mel's offices when suddenly the chauffeur pulled over to the kerb.

She knew that they had reached her destination when, clearly impatient to be rid of her—so much so that he couldn't even wait for the chauffeur to go and extract her luggage from the boot—her fellow passenger barely waited for the car to stop before he attended to that matter in person.

Since he was that keen, Delfi didn't hang about either. 'Thank you,' she said politely to the driver and exited swiftly. From there she followed the man who toted her suitcase to the door of what she only then noticed was a rather seedy-looking building. 'Thank you too,' she said sweetly, when he dropped her case down in the dark entrance hall of the building.

He grunted something—she hardly thought it was 'You're welcome'—and stepped round her to go back into the strong Bangkok sunlight.

'And that,' Delfi murmured, 'appears to be that.'

Taking up her suitcase, while absently wondering how he could have made it seem so featherlight, she went to the end of the hall. It was there that, seeing the various notices pinned to the several doors, she realised they were shared premises.

Setting her suitcase down for a moment, in the next moment she had found the door she wanted. She knocked on the door marked First Export and Import Company and, taking up her case again, she went in.

And that was when her rosy dream of working away from England, of working for Mel Dalloway in Bangkok for a year, started to come crashing down.

There was a pretty Thai girl seated over at a small telephone switchboard, but, as Delfi guessed that she must be the person who'd yesterday morning told her that Mel was out of the office, a smart but hard-looking blonde woman of about twenty-five came over to the reception desk. Her expression had been none too forthcoming before, but when she at once noticed Delfi's large suitcase—still with its airline stickers appended—her expression grew decidedly frosty.

'Yes?' she snapped, eyeing Delfi and her suitcase with the utmost suspicion.

Taken aback not only by the woman's attitude but also by the fact that she had not expected to find someone who was clearly English working there, Delfi kept her composure to state, 'I'd like to see Mr Dalloway.'

'He's been called out of town,' the woman told her without apology.

'Oh...' Delfi uttered.

'He won't be back for at least a week,' the hard-faced woman seemed to take delight in telling her.

'My name's Delfi Washington, I cabled...' Her voice faded as the hard-faced woman looked over to the young Thai receptionist and interrogated her as to whether the cable had been received.

The girl nervously agreed that the cable had been received. 'I phoned it through to Mel at——' she went on to add, but was ignored as the older woman turned her spleenish gaze back to Delfi.

'He's still not here!' she snapped.

Delfi saw the blonde's eyes again on her case and tried hard, since it looked as though she might be working with this woman, to stay friendly. 'Do you know where I can contact him?' she enquired. 'I've just flown in——'

'From England,' the woman finished for her, her tone openly hostile.

'You *do* know about me, then?' Delfi questioned, and, having expected a very different reception, she was amazed at the aggressive woman's reply.

'Like hell I do!' she snapped. 'I'm the last person that cheating rat would tell he'd got another woman on the way.'

Delfi didn't like the sound of any of this, but since she hadn't anywhere else to go she thought better than to follow her instincts and promptly get out of the grubby building. 'I'm afraid I don't understand,' she tried again to be friendly. 'I'm here to work. To——'

'So *that's* what he's calling it these days!' the blonde jeered. And as Delfi stared dumbstruck at her, 'Don't tell me, let me guess,' the woman went on, and began to mimic, '"Come and be my secretary, darling"—wasn't that the way it went when he met you in England the other week?' she asked. '"I need someone in the office who was brought up speaking English to handle the export side of things,"' she further quoted, and ended sourly, 'Sorry, ducky, you've been had!'

'Had!' Delfi exclaimed, and, while she rapidly went off all idea of working in the unsavoury surroundings, or of having this woman for an office colleague, the blonde was letting go again.

'He recruited you the same way he recruited me, didn't he?' she said, her voice rising shrilly. 'Well, tough luck on you,' she began to shout. 'In case you didn't know it, the job you were recruited for is that of Mel Dalloway's mistress and—while it suits me—that job's *mine!*'

Hardly able to believe her hearing, Delfi roused herself from her shock. 'You're welcome to it, I'm sure,' she managed to reply, but was then shaken to the very core when the blonde, having worked herself up into something of a state, lost what little veneer she had of being a lady, and began to shriek obscenities at her.

Growing paler and paler the more colourful the woman's language became, Delfi gave up all thought of trying to be friendly, or of finding out where she could contact Mel Dalloway. Feeling absolutely staggered that any woman could use such language, even though it became apparent that the woman was in love with her lover, Delfi was too stunned to consider at that point that she hadn't anywhere else to go. She was acting purely on instinct when, with the blonde still ranting foully on, she picked up her suitcase and, for once mindless of the weight of it, hurried out of the office, down the dilapidated-looking hall and out into the sunlight.

Only when she reached the pavement did Delfi put down her case, and, feeling sick to the point of wanting to vomit, she tried to surface from what had so shockingly just taken place.

She took a couple of gulped lungfuls of air as she fought to get herself back together from that dreadful scene which she had so innocently brought about. But, as she fought hard to push the memory of that woman's nauseating language from her mind, so, suddenly, Delfi began to feel quite lost and very much alone.

Even so, no matter how lost and alone she felt, nothing on God's earth would make her go back inside that building, she knew. Then, through her stewed-up thoughts and emotions, the sound of a car door being slammed angrily and forcefully penetrated.

Quickly her glance sped to where the sound had come from. Miraculously the sordid happenings of a minute or so faded from her mind when, to her amazement, she saw that the limousine she had arrived in was still stuck in traffic! But—worse than that—the man who'd met her at the airport, and who had declared that he was no friend of Mel Dalloway, had spotted her. And, much, much worse, having exited thunderously from the limousine, his expression more forbidding than ever it had been, he was striding over to where she stood!

Oh, heavens, Delfi inwardly sighed, he—*and* his hostility—were just what she didn't need right now!

CHAPTER TWO

'WHAT'S happening?' the man sharply demanded to know as he reached Delfi, there being no let-up in his enmity, or his impatience either, she observed.

But she was still feeling too shaken to be put out by whatever his attitude was. 'Precisely *nothing* is happening,' she retorted shortly. She looked at the man, whose name she still did not know, but observed that not even the heat of the day could melt the ice in those bluey green eyes.

'Where's Dalloway?' he rapped before she could draw another breath.

'I don't *know*!' Delfi told him irritably, and as agitation and anger began to turn into a combustible mix, 'Nor at the exact moment do I want to know!' she exploded.

For about a second her inquisitor stared down into her flashing violet eyes without comment. Then, after that brief pause, his expression none the warmer as he obviously realised that her plans had fallen through, 'Then what the hell am *I* supposed to do with you?' he snarled.

'You...!' Delfi exclaimed, astounded that he imagined that just because he'd met her at the airport he had to do *anything* with her! 'You don't have——' she began to tell him when, clearly a man of immediate decisions, he shot his glance from her to where the traffic had started to move again, and on that instant picked up her case and strode from her.

27

Swiftly Delfi chased after him. Then, all before she had quite realised what was going on, he had handed her case over to the chauffeur and had turned to unceremoniously "assist" her into the limousine.

By the time Delfi had got her breath back her case was reposing in the boot and the chauffeur, back behind the steering-wheel again, had the vehicle speeding along with the rest of the traffic—his destination, she gathered, being some unheard instruction the man beside her had issued.

A whole lot had taken place in Delfi's life during the past twenty-four hours. But, when it came to the most traumatic, she reckoned that the last hour took some beating. Though she was still feeling more than a degree winded by her reception at the First Export and Import Company, she was able just the same to drum up quite a dislike for the 'no time for pleasantries' aggressively silent man she was sitting next to.

When her head began to clear somewhat, however, she still had very little real idea of how she suddenly came to be riding with him in this vehicle—though she realised that maybe she should be a bit appreciative that the brute had temporarily taken charge. Whether he'd noticed that she was feeling somewhat shaken she had no idea, but he could, she belatedly realised, have ignored her and left her and her suitcase standing on the pavement. How, when her wits returned, she would have gone about getting a taxi for herself in this mad, seemingly permanent rush-hour traffic, she had no idea. Nor did she know, since she didn't know one word of Thai, how she would have made herself understood. Always supposing of course that she knew where she wanted a taxi to take her! The airport was the only place she knew.

Suddenly, then, panic descended that the airport might be the very place that this man was taking her! Whatever else she didn't know, one thing she did know, and that was that having got this far, having found the strength and everything else that had been needed to put some space between her and her sister's fiancé, she was not going to go back in a hurry—not if she could help it!

'Where are we going?' she abruptly questioned.

Idly her companion surveyed her and her obvious agitation. Then, as the car slowed and did a left turn to pull up to the entrance of a large and imposing hotel, he sharply replied, 'We're there!'

Delfi got out of the car purely and simply because one of the hotel staff had come and opened the passenger door for her and, since her escort had got out of the car at the other side, she'd have been talking to the air had she stayed put. But she didn't like it—any of it.

The hotel itself was super and she had nothing whatsoever against it—other than that it looked expensive.

'You're thinking that I'm going to stay here?' she turned to question the tall fair-haired man.

He gave her a look that endorsed the opinion she had already received—that he was cursing his tongue that he had ever said he would meet her off that plane. 'I sure as hell have no intention of driving round Bangkok with you for the rest of the day!' he fired at her acidly.

Delfi opened her mouth to give as good as she'd received, but promptly forgot what she'd meant to retaliate with when she caught sight of a hotel bellboy walking off into the hotel with her case. 'My c——' She broke off, and, looking through the plate glass to the opulent-looking interior, 'I can't afford to stay here!' she told him bluntly, hostilely.

Her hostility bounced off him. 'So give me your IOU.' He shrugged, and placed a hand under her elbow and, while a uniformed door-boy at once pulled back the plate-glass entrance, he guided her to the reception desk.

'Good morning, Mr McLaine.' A very pretty young Thai woman receptionist beamed at him, sending a gentle smile in Delfi's direction also.

'Where are *you* staying?' Delfi asked swiftly, and suspiciously, and she rapidly turned her attention to the man she now knew was called McLaine—she'd been gullible once before today in thinking she was here to work as Mel Dalloway's secretary—my giddy aunt, had she been gullible!

'Believe it or not,' McLaine drawled, 'I'm booked in here too. But,' he added, as Delfi opened her mouth to make some short and sharp protest, 'I'm just not in line for other men's cast-offs.'

With that, and while Delfi was still open-mouthed at what he had so rudely and arrogantly said, he turned to the receptionist and began booking her in. With the receptionist talking to him prettily, Delfi had better manners, as she recovered a little, than to ask to be excused while she belted Mr McLaine one for his outrageous nerve. Though she had those same good manners to thank that, with every appearance of civility, when requested she handed over her passport.

Her fury with him, however, was straining for release when, formalities completed, he turned and, passing her the room key that had just been handed to him, told her stonily, 'I've work to do,' and, to her amazement, added, 'We'll dine at eight.' Then, before Delfi could get the words out to tell him he could get lost if he thought she would voluntarily put herself in his orbit again, he had walked off towards the plate-glass doors. She was still staring after him as, the door-boy having quickly opened the doors, he went striding outside to the waiting limousine.

Well! she silently fumed, but had to forget her 'friend' McLaine for a while when the bell captain sent a porter over and Delfi saw that her case was being carried in the direction of the lifts. She followed.

Her room was twin-bedded and overlooked the Chao Phraya river, and as well as having a private safe where, had she had any valuables with her, she might keep them it also housed a refrigerator.

Delfi slipped off her shoes and at that point suddenly felt not only thirsty but extremely weary. She went over to inspect the contents of the fridge, checking the time by her watch as she did so. With a start of surprise she saw it was half-past ten—and was all at once longing to be back in England where the time was three-thirty in the morning and the rest of her family would be safely in bed.

Helping herself to a mineral water from the well-stocked fridge that held everything from lemonade to champagne, Delfi took her drink with her to one of the beds and, propping herself up on the pillows, knew that she needed to think.

The trouble with that, however, was that, having slept barely at all on Sunday night and having slept not one wink on the plane, she now felt thoroughly exhausted. So exhausted did she in fact feel that nothing very brilliant was getting through. Mel Dalloway had not met her at the airport as promised, but he had clearly received her cable and had been expecting her, or why else arrange for her to be met? But, as to the existence of a job, Delfi reckoned that—with or without that foul-mouthed woman as a colleague—she could forget about any sort of a job at First Export and Import Company.

Delfi's eyelids began to droop as one fact above all others set like concrete in her mind: that having for good reasons left England for what she had grown to think would be for about a year, and having made the break, there was no way she was going to return any earlier. Not if she could help it anyway.

She awoke to find that it was dusk and hurriedly switched on the light to see that she must have gone sound out for seven solid hours, because it was now six o'clock.

Her surprise about that, however, soon diminished, and with nothing to charge around for she left her bed to go and stare out of the window of her eighteenth-floor room down at the river and the various craft going back and forth.

All too soon, though, memories of the predicament she was in arrived to prevent her from taking more than scant pleasure from the scene set out below. She came away from the window with one thought still dominating her mind—she just could *not* return to England.

How, without the First Export and Import job to keep her in funds, that was to be achieved occupied all of Delfi's thinking as she went and undid her case. She had drawn out all her savings from the building society so had enough money for her immediate needs, she calculated as she found her toilet bag and took some fresh clothes from her case. Since it was dark now it seemed common sense to stay the one night in this hotel, but she would most definitely have to do something about finding somewhere cheaper in the morning, she realised. She hung up the dress she would later change into in the wardrobe, then she discovered a freshly laundered towelling robe, courtesy of the hotel. She broke the paper band around it and took the robe with her into the bathroom.

By the time she emerged from the bathroom one Mr Surly-brute McLaine had entered her thoughts. She tried to oust him; she had quite sufficient to think of without remembering that lordly swine with his bossy edict 'We'll dine at eight.' He could go and take a running jump for a start. It was for sure, though, that, while she was desperately scratching around for some idea that would somehow make the impossibility of eking out her limited funds for a year a possibility, that arrogant creature would have no such problem. Aside from the fact that his clothes and shoes were of the best quality, there was something about him—without the fact that he was staying in this expensive hotel—that proclaimed that *he* wasn't short of funds.

At around seven-thirty she left her room and, feeling hungry, decided to investigate if the hotel had a coffee shop where she could perhaps get a sandwich to keep her going until she found somewhere cheaper tomorrow.

She had been allowed to bring only a small amount of Thai currency into the country with her, but took note when she reached the ground-floor area that she could change some of her traveller's cheques into Thai baht in the hotel.

Perhaps she'd do that a little later on, she mused, and while investigating where there might be a coffee shop she found a shop that sold picture postcards and realised that her very first job must be to send a card home.

'Do you have stamps too?' she asked the smiling, English-speaking young woman who served her.

'The concierge will have stamps,' she was informed, and Delfi, having exchanged some of her baht for a postcard, went and found a place to write her 'everything terrific' report without actually lying, and from there went to the concierge's desk.

It was there that, having just posted her card, she was joined by a tall fair-haired man whom she knew to be English. To her chagrin, though, it seemed he quite confidently believed she was hanging around for him when he commented, 'Good. You're on time.'

Delfi opened her mouth to smartly set him straight, then most oddly found she was holding back on acid, in favour of sarcasm. 'I should hate to keep you waiting,' she murmured, her violet eyes wide and innocent—and discovered that her sarcasm was totally ignored.

Either that or McLaine was too full of himself to consider that she might not be falling over herself to have him take her to dinner. And that made her cross, especially when, giving her no more than a curt glance, he grunted, 'This way.'

Her acid so very nearly made it that time. Then suddenly the notion swiftly jetted in that, since he seemed to be a man who knew his way about, he might be able to advise her on where she might find some inexpensive hotel or even pension—if they had that sort of thing in Thailand.

For that reason alone, Delfi swallowed down the crossness she felt, and went with him to an elegant restaurant where, clearly expected, he was courteously greeted by a smiling head waiter.

In no time at all they were seated at a secluded table for two, with Delfi feeling as cool towards the man she knew only as McLaine as the hard-at-work air-conditioning was keeping the dining-room.

When the waiter handed her the menu she silently studied it while forming the opinion that, since McLaine clearly wasn't the 'chatty' type, it was going to be some fun mealtime.

'I'll have tomato soup,' she told the attentive waiter, and—defiantly when she caught her host's cynical look, which she was positive said, My, my, aren't we the adventurous type?—she went on, 'and I'll have...' She broke off, then read from the menu, '*Gai phad ma-*

muang him-ma-phan, to follow.' What McLaine ordered, she didn't care to note.

What she did note some minutes later, however—indeed, could hardly fail to miss—was that her earlier sarcasm, though to all intents and purposes ignored, had very definitely been spotted.

Their first course had been consumed with barely any conversation passing between them. Delfi had just started on her second course, though, when she suddenly found out that any notion she'd nursed that Thai food would be fairly bland was totally misconceived. *Gai phad ma-muang him-ma-phan* turned out to be nothing more alarming than sautéd chicken with cashew nuts. When Delfi put a forkful of what she thought were accompanying black mushrooms into her mouth, however, and the hot spice flavour hit her, she was left gasping for breath.

Instinctively she sent her shaken gaze to the man opposite, and found herself staring into cool, sardonic blue-green eyes. Indolently he called the waiter over, and as the man went swiftly to do his bidding he drawled mockingly, 'Dare we hope, Miss Washington, that the black peppers are burning some of the sarcasm off your pretty little tongue?' While Delfi stared at him and felt that if she weren't so otherwise preoccupied now might be a nice moment to attempt to box his ears, the waiter arrived swiftly with a glass of mineral water.

Gratefully she took the glass from him, but only when she had downed half of it did she turn on her host and accuse, 'You *knew*!'

'True.' He shrugged, it clearly being entirely immaterial to him that she had burned her mouth on the spices.

'You might have told me!' she snapped.

'Aside from the fact that I thought everyone knew that Thai food is well spiced, I rather gained the impression that any warning I gave would have been ignored,' he tossed at her coldly.

He was right there, Delfi supposed with reluctant honesty. Having ordered what she had, she knew enough about herself, and the hostility this man aroused in her, to know that sheer bravado would have had her thumbing her nose at any kind of warning he might have uttered.

She took up her fork again, and the rest of her meal was quite delicious. She popped a morsel of chicken into her mouth and realised that, as she had done with the spiciness of her main course as a subject, McLaine certainly had too.

It was time, Delfi decided, to endeavour to get near to the question she wanted to ask about less expensive accommodation. It occurred to her that, by virtue of the fact that she was sitting here sharing a meal with him, she must have accepted his invitation to dine. Now seemed the right moment to bring out a few social graces and act the part of a well-mannered guest.

'Do you reside permanently in Bangkok?' she swallowed any remaining ire to ask politely.

If he considered her question unexpected, he didn't show it, but had her ire straining for release when, after favouring her coolly with a long, speculative look, 'No,' he replied briefly.

To her way of thinking, social graces were a two-way street. But since she still wanted to put the 'alternative accommodation' question to him she swallowed more irritation and enquired in her best-brought-up manner, 'Is Mrs McLaine not travelling with you this trip, Mr McLaine?'

Again he looked at her long and levelly, but stretched to the limits Delfi's recently awakened urge to set about him when he replied, 'My mother is in England. So, as far as I know, is my father's second wife. As, too, is Gina, my father's present wife.'

'Good—heavens!' Delfi gasped faintly, her surprise at learning that, apparently, McLaine senior had a penchant for marrying not once but three times nullifying her initial annoyance that the offspring of that first marriage was deliberately not answering what she thought was a perfectly natural question. 'Er—you're not married yourself?' she recovered to rephrase her original question—and wished she hadn't when his right eyebrow flicked up a fraction, and she had the most dreadful feeling that he was assessing what was behind her question. 'Obviously I'm not interested personally,' she hastened to tell him, starting to feel dreadful suddenly in case he should think she was setting her cap at him—and his wallet.

'Good,' he replied shortly, and with what she saw as straight-from-the-shoulder honesty he laid on the line, 'With a record like my father's before me, I decided some while ago that marriage is something I don't need.'

'Nothing like being positive,' Delfi muttered, starting to positively loathe him—as if she needed warning off, for goodness' sake! Grief, with the minimum of luck she wouldn't see the overbearing brute again—once this meal was finished. Which reminded her, she had a question she wanted to ask him before they went their separate ways. Though, since he was not a Bangkok resident, it suddenly seemed less likely now that he would have the answer. 'You're here on holiday?' she remained outwardly civil to enquire.

'With some work thrown in,' he answered aloofly, when she had begun to think that he wouldn't answer at all.

As Delfi belatedly remembered how McLaine had that morning left her with the words, 'I've work to do,' so

the waiter came to their table and cleared away their
second course, and asked what they would like for
dessert. This time, regardless of any derisory glance she
might or might not receive from her host, Delfi ordered
a cherry strudel.

Her strudel had arrived and she was just about to cut
into it, however, when she suddenly discovered that her
curiosity about the man opposite had a will of its own.
For, quite without meaning to, and his remark about
'work' the culprit, she realised, she found she was asking,
'Do you work in export and import too?'

'Too?' he queried.

'The same as Mel Dalloway,' she replied, adding
quickly when she saw that Mel's name didn't seem to
be going down very well, 'Despite what you said about
his not being a friend of yours, he must be. You——'

'Your charm, Miss Washington, is something else
again,' he grated.

'What do you mean by that?' she quickly erupted.

'It's not every day I get called a liar!' he rapped.

'Oh,' she said faintly, only then realising that by insisting that he must be a friend of Mel Dalloway's, when
he had firmly told her that he was not, she had more or
less called him a liar. 'But you know him,' she drew fresh
breath to argue. 'You met me at the airport this morning
on his behalf, so——'

'I've never met the man,' he sliced through what she
was saying, and consequently had her staring at him in
disbelief. 'I met you on my father's behalf, no one else's,'
he went on to announce flatly.

'Your—father!' Delfi exclaimed, and stared at him in
total mystification.

That she was quite bewildered by what he had just
said must have got through to him, she realised. Because—when she would have laid odds against it—he

was suddenly unbending sufficiently to detail, 'I was unaware of Dalloway's—or your—existence when I went with my father to the airport to see him off this morning.' Delfi remained bewildered. 'Because of the traffic we were late getting there, and what with my father having other problems on his mind, he was almost on his way when he suddenly remembered he'd given his word to Dalloway that he'd meet your plane.'

'Oh—so—it's your father who's a friend of Mel Dalloway?' Delfi inserted—that bit seemed clear.

'If you can call an acquaintanceship as recent as early yesterday evening friendship,' McLaine retorted shortly, but added drily, 'My father, with his love of all humanity, has a mammoth propensity for picking up strays.'

'Strays!' she echoed, never having thought of Mel Dalloway as a stray, if that was whom he was referring to.

It proved that it was when, as if she hadn't spoken, McLaine went on, 'My father was in Bangkok with me while I put in some time at an exhibition here. He'd spent an hour with me there yesterday afternoon and in the early evening wandered off to one of the bars where he apparently struck up an acquaintance with Dalloway.'

'I see,' Delfi murmured, though that they'd all been at the same exhibition at the same time was about the only thing that she did see.

'They subsequently shared a few beers, during which time my father revealed that while I was again going to be occupied at the exhibition today he himself had nothing very pressing he had to attend to.'

'Ah . . . !' Delfi exclaimed, as light started to filter in.

'Exactly,' McLaine acknowledged briefly, and completed, 'Dalloway, jokingly at first, I believe, then suggested that, since he was tied up and couldn't make it personally, my father could do him a great favour if he'd care to meet your plane.'

'And your father, with his love of all humanity—not forgetting his mammoth propensity for picking up strays—agreed,' Delfi took up sharply, ignoring the acid look McLaine threw her. She wasn't too thrilled herself to find she was now included under the 'strays' heading also!

'He naturally said he'd be charmed,' her dinner companion relayed coldly.

It was for sure the son had inherited none of the father's charm, Delfi thought sourly as she took up her spoon and sampled her cherry strudel. But her intelligence was at work, and it was but a moment later that she flicked a glance at the man who had come off badly when sweetness and light had been handed out, and questioned, 'But talk of airports later made your father decide to take a plane somewhere himself—thereby making it impossible for him to meet me as he'd told Mel Dalloway he would?'

McLaine shook his head. 'He had every intention of meeting you until early this morning he had a frantic phone call from his present wife to say that one of his stepchildren had been injured in an accident.'

'Oh—I see,' Delfi murmured slowly, and thought she really did see as she continued, 'Naturally your father said he'd return home straight away but, worried and no doubt in a rush, he was almost on the plane before he remembered me.'

'That's about it,' McLaine agreed. 'Just in time he remembered his promise and how your plane must have landed about half an hour previously. He then gave me a lightning outline of what had happened, added your name and that of Dalloway—the rest,' he ended, 'you know.'

Didn't she just. If it hadn't been for McLaine keeping his father's promise for him she'd have been left hanging around for goodness knew how long. It was quite probable that any phone call she'd made from the airport to First Export and Import Company would have been intercepted by the blonde, and would have been uncooperatively dealt with.

'I suppose,' Delfi owned with what she admitted was a fair amount of reluctance, 'that I must thank you.'

'Huh!' he scoffed, and entirely uninterested in her polite mouthing, 'Keep your begrudging thanks!'

Delfi did not take kindly to having her statement of gratitude flung back at her—even if her thanks had been reluctantly given—and she flared, 'Are you always so disagreeable?'

'Most of the time!' he bit back. But, looking angrily at him, Delfi with a jolt could have sworn that she caught a glimpse of humour lurking. Not that he allowed it to see the light of day, and after another watchful second Delfi returned her attention to her pudding.

It wasn't too long, however, when, having gone over some of what had been said, she realised that she owed McLaine more than begrudging thanks. She took another spoonful of cherry strudel, knowing by then that thanks were due to him not only for meeting her but for seeing to it that she had a roof over her head that night. He needn't have done that when he'd come over to her on that pavement outside Mel Dalloway's offices, she realised. His promise to his father to meet her had been kept, his duty done.

She looked up, and wanted to thank him more sincerely, but at his cold stare the words got stuck in her throat. Then the moment when she might have tried anyway was lost when, 'Coffee?' he enquired with a flicked glance down to her cleared plate.

'Thanks,' she replied, and left it at that.

Coffee had arrived and Delfi was taking a first ex-
perimental sip of hers when, somewhat to her surprise,
though with his tone no more affable than it had been,
McLaine leaned back in his chair to idly enquire, 'So
how did you come to meet Dalloway?'

'I met him at a party in London,' she saw no harm
in revealing, but since she had not the smallest incli-
nation to talk about herself or Mel Dalloway either for
that matter, 'Do you and your father normally live in
England?' she politely asked to change the conversation.

'Normally,' he replied, but from the speculative look
he tossed her Delfi had a clear impression that any questions McLaine wanted to ask had only been put on temporary hold.

'Er—you and your father are in the same business?'
she queried nicely, guilt about her reluctant thanks
making her feel that perhaps it was time that she made
an effort in the manners department.

'My father wouldn't recognise an engineering instrument if it rose up and bit him,' McLaine enlightened
her. 'He's an anthropologist.'

'Oh,' she murmured, and, since, she'd started this,
felt she had to go on, 'But you're an engineer?'

Over the next couple of minutes, and in the fewest
words possible, McLaine supplied the briefest outline of
what work he did. Delfi still had the feeling that he was
only biding his time to get a few questions of his own
in as she sifted through what he had told her to conclude
that he was the owner of McLaine International, a very
high-tech firm of instrument manufacturers.

'It—sounds most interesting,' she commented when
she realised that that was all that he was going to tell
her.

He shrugged, then, after looking at her for a long moment or two, he revealed, 'I made a few enquiries about Dalloway today.'

'What sort of enquiries?' she asked sharply.

He walked through her question as if she hadn't asked it. 'You knew, of course, that he's married?'

'Married!' she exclaimed, remembering how in London Mel Dalloway's main aim had seemed to be to try and get her to go to bed with him. 'I can hardly credit it!' she gasped.

McLaine did not argue the point, but, just as though he believed it as gospel, 'He was your lover in London,' he stated.

'That he wasn't!' Delfi declared stoutly.

She was still staring at McLaine with angry, flashing eyes when his all-assessing look at the vehemence of her denial suddenly alerted to take on a sharper edge. Then slowly, with nothing in any way hurried about him, 'Ye gods,' he softly drawled, 'are you still wet behind the ears?'

Delfi knew exactly what he meant, and did not pretend otherwise. Though she had a job to make her voice as offhand as she would have liked when she replied, 'That's one quaint way of putting it!'

'Why?' he questioned, his tone suddenly sharp again, but Delfi resented his questioning. Surely it was up to her whether she lost or retained her virginity?

'Why not?' she tossed back at him.

McLaine inclined his head a touch as he sombrely surveyed her. Then, his aggression never very far from the surface as far as she could tell, he abruptly snarled, 'What the hell—given your preference for a solitary bed—are you doing here?'

Her breath was taken for a moment at the sheer aggression in the man, and Delfi threw him a look of thorough dislike. Heavens, surely there had to be more to life than jumping in and out of bed with every man one met—hadn't there? 'I came here,' she told him stiffly, 'to work!' There, she thought, make something out of that. She was very much annoyed when he did.

He gave her a long level look, then, somehow knowing that there was more behind it than that—though how he knew she didn't have the first idea—he asked the blunt question, 'Why?'

Delfi had never met a man like him, nor did she want to ever again. 'That's my business!' she hissed, and suddenly felt pushed to add, her tone grown as aggressive as his, 'I suppose you do have a first name?'

Blue-green eyes were fixed on her silver-blonde hair and violet eyes when, not one whit put out by her swift change of subject matter, he leaned back to let fall, 'Boden.'

That was all Delfi waited to hear. In the next second she was on her feet. She had her shoulder-bag hanging off her shoulder when, 'Then goodbye, Mr McLaine!' she told him furiously, and marched out of there.

CHAPTER THREE

By THE time Delfi had reached her room she was very much regretting her reply to Boden McLaine's question of why she had come here to Bangkok to work. Why couldn't she have told him that she had simply felt like a change, or invented one of a dozen or so equally simple explanations? With her reply of 'That's my business', all she'd succeeded in doing was to give him cause to know that he was right to think there was some deeper reason at the back of it.

She let herself into her room to suddenly realise that McLaine very probably wouldn't give her or her reasons for leaving England another thought. Hugh Renshaw—and her merciless companion 'guilt' about him—was the reason she had given Boden McLaine that aggressive reply, she saw. But he was a businessman, for goodness' sake, here on business. He certainly had better things to do than to waste time in thinking about her reasons.

Thoughts of Boden McLaine or Hugh Renshaw all at once went winging from her mind as she noticed that someone had been to her room. A smile of pleasure curved her beautiful mouth on going over to her bed, as she saw the purple orchid that was now, courtesy of the hotel, nestling on her pillow. That was not the only courtesy the hotel provided, she observed, for there on a low table was a basket of fresh, cellophane-wrapped fruit.

Her pleasure at these attentions, however, was doomed not to last for long. How could it when she was soon back to thinking of her abrupt departure from McLaine and how she had never got around to asking him if he had any idea where she might find some respectable but inexpensive lodgings?

Such worrying thoughts occupied her as she hung up a fresh and smart day dress from her case that she would wear tomorrow and pottered around. When later she prepared for bed all her worry had brought her not a step nearer to knowing what she was going to do.

She got into bed having been over again all the inner turmoil she had been through over her sister's fiancé, and knew that she just *couldn't* go home for it to start all over again. She had made the break—she just *couldn't* go back.

Strangely, when Hugh Renshaw had occupied a lot of her thinking, it was not of him that she thought when she eventually closed her eyes, but Boden McLaine. He was a brute of a man, she firmly decided, yet she thought she had detected in him the faint glimmerings of a sense of humour. A smile tugged at the corners of her mouth when, just before sleep claimed her, it then struck her as slightly amusing that she had asked him his first name and then, to show how unfriendly she felt towards him, had called him Mr McLaine.

Amusement was far from her when she awakened the next morning and the worries of the previous evening awakened with her. She left her comfortable bed wondering where she would be laying her head that night— it was certain that it wouldn't be here.

It was still early when, showered and dressed, she decided she had better get on with her day as soon as possible. On thinking about it, it seemed sensible to go down and partake of something solid in the way of breakfast to start her day, and then return to her room to collect her belongings.

Remembering to take her room key, Delfi opened her door and discovered that looped over the doorknob at the other side, in a neat transparent plastic wrapper, was a copy of the independent Thai newspaper called the *Nation*. Since it was printed in English she took it with her, and descended in one of the lifts to find that, as early as it was, there were plenty of people milling around.

From the plethora of briefcases, they were mainly business people, she noted as she went into the self-service breakfast-room and found a table. Bangkok, she realised, was clearly an important business city.

She was tucking into scrambled eggs with her thoughts miles away when she suddenly became aware of a business-suited European two tables away blatantly giving her encouraging looks.

Spare me! she thought in disgust and, to show just how interested she was in a breakfast-time flirtation, she took the *Nation* out of its plastic bag and took pleasure in ignoring him. The paper came in several sections, she observed, and opted to immerse herself in the 'Focus' section first.

Soon, however, when Delfi had only picked up the paper in order to better ignore the unwanted attention of a visiting Casanova, her attention was riveted. Here—to her gigantic relief she found she had turned to a Job Opportunities column—was the obvious answer! Oh, why hadn't she thought of it for herself? Where had her head been? Hadn't she come here to work? What was more natural than, the one job proving non-existent, she should look for some other paid employment to keep her afloat?

'Secretary wanted,' she read, 'good command of English and English typing.' She stopped reading that one when she saw it ended, 'Must speak Thai.' She switched to another advert requesting jewellery sales staff. The problem with that one was the final, 'Must speak Japanese.'

Undaunted, Delfi was deeply engrossed in other adverts under the Job Opportunities heading when a voice over her shoulder enquired coolly, 'You do have a work permit, of course?'

She'd know that voice anywhere! Somehow, though, she had never expected to see Boden McLaine again. She looked up, saw him tall, immaculate in his light-weight business suit, and disliked him afresh because when there had appeared to be a sliver of light on her dark horizon, he was trying to take that light from her. She gave him a speaking look, and didn't like him any better when, by the look of it intending to share her table, he propped his briefcase on a spare chair and went off in the direction of the self-service area.

That she did *not* have a work permit was mainly down to Mel Dalloway's confident 'Just hop on a jumbo' making it seem that there was little more to it than that. Perhaps she *would* have thought about it if she hadn't got so much else on her mind, but because of Mel's confidence, coupled with the fact that First Export and Import Company was a British firm and she a British citizen, she hadn't given the matter any thought. She was sure though that she'd put 'working' on her visa application as the reason for wanting to come to Thailand. Or—suddenly Delfi began to doubt that fact— had she, fresh from the travel agent who'd gone on and on about touring, accidently put 'touring' as her reason?

Delfi had discovered that she just couldn't remember when, without so much as a by-your-leave, Boden McLaine returned to set his breakfast down opposite her.

He reached for the cruet. 'You haven't, have you?' he enquired, just as if five minutes hadn't elapsed since he'd asked the question.

'I'm sure I won't need one!' she told him with confidence that was more assumed than actual.

Casually, he returned the cruet from whence it came, then, his voice the pleasantest she had yet heard it, 'Ever seen the inside of a Thai gaol?' he enquired, all charm.

Pig, she thought, certain, while she held down alarm, that working without a permit couldn't be that serious as to warrant a gaol sentence. 'I'm sure Thai gaols are quite nice,' she replied coolly, and finding what confidence she could, 'Though I shouldn't think it will be too difficult for me to obtain a permit to work.'

'You intend to stay on?' he rapped.

His charm hadn't stayed around long, Delfi noted as she heard the blunt aggression in his voice with which she was more familiar. 'It ... would ... suit me—to stay on for a while,' she told him arrogantly, if a degree or two falteringly.

'Are you in some sort of trouble back home?' he at once sliced through her arrogance to demand.

'Certainly not!' Delfi retorted smartly, and glared at him.

Much good did it do her. For, ever a man to cut one down to size, and all too obviously having not forgotten her statement of yesterday morning when she'd told him that she could not afford to stay in this hotel, 'Just how do you propose to exist while waiting for a permit?' he further challenged.

If she knew herself she certainly wouldn't tell him, Delfi thought furiously. But, as her spirits dipped at the way he made it sound as though it would take forever for a work permit to come through, she had the hardest work in the world to keep her hostility going when, 'At the risk of being repetitive,' she retorted cuttingly, 'that's *my* business!'

Oh, grief, she thought when his brow darkened in displeasure, he wasn't liking her attitude one tiny bit. It was plain to her then that, his expression arctic, he was about to tell her to go to the devil.

To her complete surprise, however, he said nothing of the sort, but, his jaw jerking, 'When you accepted my help yesterday,' he gritted, 'you made it mine!' Delfi was still staring at him in amazement that he should think he need take any responsibility for her when, after a pause of great mutual dislike, he spoke again. 'Can you type?' he barked—as if against his will.

'I'm a trained secretary,' she answered tartly, having not the first clue what tack he was on now but wishing that he'd clear off and leave her to get on with her day. Silence fell as his eyes raked her dainty features, and, 'Why?' she found herself breaking the antagonistic silence to do a little demanding in return.

'Because I might have a use for your services, that's why!' he slammed back at her.

'My secretarial services?' she, who'd been caught napping once before, remained belligerent to demand.

The look of dislike he threw her would have curdled milk. He had no need to add anything for her to get the picture that he liked his women with a more pleasing personality than she had—but of course he did. 'Forgive me for being blunt,' he rapped icily, looking anything but sorry, 'but even *should* I fancy you——' a fair hint there that margarine would turn to butter before that happened '—I've never paid for *those* kind of services—nor do I intend to start!'

'W...' Outraged by what he had said, Delfi was just about to go into verbal orbit when a waiter came to their table and poured fresh coffee. By the time the waiter

had gone, what else Boden McLaine had said had sep-
arated itself from the rest of it. With the operative word
being 'pay', Delfi realised that he'd just said that he
would *pay* her to do some work for him. With some
difficulty, she swallowed her ire. 'I—er—was more than
a little credulous a couple of days ago when I left England
thinking I was coming to Bangkok to work as Mel
Dalloway's secretary—when it seems all he wanted was
another mistress,' she announced, what she'd said the
best she could do by way of an apology for her sus-
picious nature.

She took a glance to Boden McLaine; his eyes were
steady on her, she observed. But, to her relief, his tone
was much milder than it had been. 'What are your family
thinking of, letting you loose?' he wanted to know.

'I'm twenty-two!' she replied stiffly, at once resenting
any criticism of her family.

'I'm fast realising that there's twenty-two and twenty-
two!' he retorted. And before she could take any great
exception to that, 'You must have an attending angel
watching over you,' he suddenly pronounced. 'From a
phone conversation I had with my father a couple of
hours ago, it seems I should have not only met you yesterday, but delivered you to a "non-office" address which
Dalloway had given him.'

'A non...' All this was news to her. 'But——'

'My father had a lot on his mind when he left yesterday,' Boden McLaine slotted in.

'He only remembered at the last moment that he'd
said he'd meet me,' Delfi recalled.

Boden McLaine nodded. 'So it's no surprise that he
should forget to give me the address.'

'Do you—er—have it—the address?' she enquired
tentatively, thoughts of her need for alternative accommodation ever present.

'No, I don't!' he exploded categorically, and her eyes shot wide to hear his aggression out in full force again. 'Ye gods!' he rapped furiously. 'You're *surely* not thinking of taking up Dalloway's——?'

'Of course not!' she erupted hotly. 'Grief,' she simmered down to add, 'before you'd told me he was married I'd heard enough from the present mistress incumbent at that office you took me to yesterday to know that, not only is there no job for me there, but Mel Dalloway is nothing but a "no slightest chance let by" womaniser.' She paused for breath. 'I——' she began again, but Boden McLaine interrupted.

'Rough, was it?' he asked kindly, and, as if he was remembering how shaken she'd looked when she'd reeled out of the First Export and Import Company, his expression seemed much less harsh.

'I...' she said again, but to her horror, maybe because she had never expected him to have a softer side, a more sensitive side, she discovered that she was on the very brink of tears! Swiftly she looked down to her plate. Then, 'I need some marmalade,' she told the pink linen tablecloth, and in the next moment she had left her chair and was heading to the self-service area.

Delfi was in no hurry to return to the table she had left so abruptly. She had realised a couple of things though when—since to pick up a pre-packed helping of marmalade couldn't take all day—she started to make her way back. One thing she realised was that her emotions must be exceedingly raw that she should feel like bursting into tears at the first kind word she should hear from McLaine. The other thing she realised was that, from what she had learned of the man in the short time since she had known him, any stray kinder streak that had surfaced in him just wouldn't stay around for long.

He was busy drinking a fresh cup of coffee as she placed the marmalade on the table and retook her seat. She had, by then, got herself back together again and was going over what had sounded like talk of a job offer. If she could work for that awful Mr Yardley of Kenyon Cylinders, then she could work for anybody, she decided—even McLaine when he reverted to being a monster—as without doubt he would.

'You—er—intimated you'd pay me to be your secretary,' she suddenly broke into speech, and for a moment, as Boden McLaine put down his coffee-cup and then surveyed her from across the table, she feared that she had left it too late and that the job trail had gone cold.

She was much relieved, therefore, when, after some moments, he clarified, 'Temporary secretary.'

Temporary was better than nothing in her book. 'Of course,' she murmured, and to give him a taste of her intelligence, 'I don't suppose the exhibition will be on for much longer.'

'It ends on Saturday,' he replied, and, while her spirits sank because when she'd hoped to have a minimum of two weeks' work it looked as though she'd be lucky to have as many as four days' paid employment, he was going on, 'But the work I want you to do is totally unconnected with the exhibition.'

'It—is?' Delfi queried slowly.

'My father, as I've mentioned, is an anthropologist,' he began to clarify some more. 'The original idea of his coming to Thailand with me was for him to have a holiday in Bangkok while the exhibition is on. Then for me to accompany him up north where I would holiday while he did some research into the advantages and disadvantages experienced by the hill tribes since civilisation—of a sort—has caught up with them.'

'Oh!' Delfi exclaimed in mild, but interested surprise. 'But your father had to cut short his holiday when one of his stepchildren had an accident and he had to leave in a hurry.'

'Though not before saying that he would be back by Saturday so we should continue as planned. His phone call this morning changed all that.'

'He found his stepchild was worse than he'd anticipated?'

'His wife needs him.' Boden McLaine shrugged, and left that part of it there, to go on, 'The upshot of his call, since he can't get back as arranged, and since—as he in his parental way pointed out— I shall still be on holiday as planned, seems to be that I've agreed to go and do the research for him.'

'You're going up north?' Delfi checked.

'That's right.'

'You're suggesting that I as your secretary—temporary secretary,' she amended hastily, 'come too?'

'You'll hardly be any good to me here!' he grunted, starting to get a shade irritated with her, she saw.

'How long will we be there?' she quickly asked, now not the time to look a gift horse in the mouth.

'Given that I'm not even an amateur anthropologist, let alone a professional one, it should take a year. But,' he said flatly, 'a month is all I can spare.'

A month's paid work at that stage was like manna from heaven to her, and Delfi hurriedly sifted through what he had told her. The only problem though, she quickly saw, was that if she was away in the north, then it ruled out her being on hand in Bangkok to look for other work or attend to the—by the sound of it—drawn-out business of obtaining a work permit. Also——

'Well?' The grim sound of Boden McLaine's enquiry sliced harshly through her speculations. 'Do you want the job or not?' he rapped, clearly a man who had better things to do than to sit patiently waiting while she thought about it.

Delfi knew then that since she wasn't going to get a better offer she'd better buck her ideas up and grab at the chance of the job before he changed his mind. 'When do I start?' she accepted. He still didn't look overjoyed, she observed.

'I've work to do here first,' he said curtly, and, to Delfi's mind too bossy by far, even if he was now, technically speaking, her boss, he instructed, 'Consider yourself on standby until my business here is complete.'

'How long will that take?' she dug her toes in to pleasantly enquire, as a stubbornness not to be intimidated by his arrogant manner suddenly stirred.

'When the exhibition ends, so will my stint in Bangkok,' he tossed at her.

Saturday, in fact, she saw. 'You'll need my secretarial services during that time?'

'I've all the help I need on the exhibition side,' he replied.

Which, Delfi realised, was logical since he'd not needed a secretary for the business he was here in Bangkok to do before she'd arrived. But she had one very pressing problem forever nipping at her heels, and quickly, before pride would make her duck it, she hurriedly asked, 'What about my accommodation until then? I can afford one night here,' she told him with swift honesty, 'but any more and——'

'Since it was I who booked you into this hotel, and since you are now in my employ, your hotel bill is my concern,' he cut in, and, all hard-headed businessman suddenly, he went on to state matter-of-factly how much he was going to pay her. Delfi was still taking in the generous amount and was realising that whatever else

he was he was no cheapskate when, as if he considered
that he had spent more than enough time on this discussion, he caught hold of his briefcase, and stood up.
'That covers everything. Goodbye, Miss Washington.'
He nodded, and before she could blink he had gone
about his business.

Delfi was still where Boden McLaine had left her some
five minutes later. By then she had come to the firm
conclusion that her new employer was most definitely
something of an enigma. Brute, monster, and acid
enough to have lived his whole life on a diet of citrus
certainly. But, that notwithstanding, she had once
thought she'd seen a hint that he had a sense of humour,
and could he be all monster when, from what he'd said,
it seemed that he was prepared to give up his planned
holiday to do some work for his father?

They'd both been going up north, Delfi remembered
as she left her seat and went in the direction of the hotel
cashier's clerk. So perhaps it wasn't any hardship for
Boden McLaine—having found a secretary to assist him
with work he was unfamiliar with—to agree to his
father's request. He would be on holiday, true, but since
the work with the hill tribes would be vastly different
from his more normal work the rest from engineering
would perhaps still constitute a holiday.

'Can I change a traveller's cheque?' she enquired of
the cashier.

'Certainly, madam,' the cashier smiled, and as he
busied himself with her request Delfi fell to wondering
how the three-times-married McLaine senior had
managed to leave his family ties for so long as he'd
planned.

He hadn't though, had he? she realised a moment later.
He'd received an urgent summons home and, once there,
had found the present Mrs McLaine had need of him,

either because of the seriousness of the injury to her child or, as Delfi was beginning to suspect, because she hadn't cared for her husband—with his track record of marriages—going off for what must be over a month.

Whatever, Delfi realised as she put her newly exchanged Thai baht away, she reckoned she had the present Mrs McLaine to thank that she now had what looked like a month's paid employment in front of her.

Delfi was back in her room when it suddenly began to dawn on her that, since it didn't look as if she'd have very much to pay in the way of outgoing expenses in the next four to five weeks, she'd have quite a few baht to tide her over at the end of that time. Sufficient anyway to make it not so pressing as it had been for her to find a job to start as immediately as the day after her stint for Boden McLaine had ended.

On the strength of that thought, Delfi all at once and for the first time in an age started to feel a little easier in her mind. With innate fairness, she realised that the fact she should suddenly start to feel less strained was all down to Boden McLaine and his job offer—even if she still wasn't liking him very much. He had said nothing about seeing her at dinner though, so presumably, since he knew where to contact her, he would if he had any news to impart do so between now and when she took up her secretarial duties proper.

Why she should trust him after the way Mel Dalloway—with his non-existent job—had let her down, Delfi could not have said. She remembered his strong no-nonsense manner, however, and knew that, with that nebulous something about him that just shouted integrity, trust him she did.

She glanced to the window and only then noticed that it was a beautiful sunny day outside, and forgot for the moment any urgency she had felt to begin looking into

how one went about obtaining a work permit. Life had
been hell recently, but the sun was shining—did life have
to be hell all the time?

Before she could change her mind, Delfi grabbed up
her bag and left her room. She did not want to spend
the whole of the day hanging around the hotel on the
vague possibility that Boden McLaine might need her—
surely he would not expect her to!

She had no clear idea of quite where she was going
when she stepped outside the hotel, but, since she all at
once felt quite flush with baht, when a taxi stopped
straight in front of her it seemed an opportunity not to
miss.

So, too, thought another resident of the hotel, she realised, but a second later, for as she went to get into the
taxi a tall youth of about twenty loped up to her.

'Where are you going?' he asked, English himself and
taking her for belonging to the same nation.

'The Grand Palace.' Delfi, in her surprise, brought
out the name that had been on the picture postcard she
had written home last evening.

'So am I,' he replied. 'Want to share?'

Since he was obviously staying at the same expensive
hotel that she was, Delfi did not suppose for a moment
that he was short of the taxi fare. But, as flush with baht
as she now considered herself to be, it seemed quite a
sensible thing to do.

'Of course,' she agreed, finding nothing in any way
offensive in the fresh-faced young man.

By the time the taxi dropped them off at the white
and gold Grand Palace, Delfi had exchanged names with
her fellow passenger, and had learned that Kevin Carroll
was a student from Devizes who'd been having a hard
time at university. He told her he was, at his under-
standing parents' suggestion, having a couple of weeks

off during which time he was to decide whether or not he left university permanently.

Delfi found him no trouble at all to get along with and they fell into step, as far as they might with the area being so crowded, and wandered around together.

Kevin, she discovered, was a camera buff. 'Aw—that's disappointing!' he exclaimed when, having removed their shoes and entered the chapel of the famed statue of national veneration, the Emerald Buddha, he discovered that he was not permitted to take photographs inside.

All was not lost, they later found, for on leaving the chapel and going round to the front he spotted an open window looking in straight on to the Emerald Buddha. Photography was allowed there and Delfi went to put her shoes on while he joined the rest of the camera-keen fraternity.

He was all smiles when he came over to where she was. 'Fancy coming to find a lemonade or something?' he asked.

It was swelteringly hot. 'Sounds like a good idea,' Delfi agreed, and went with him in search of something thirst-quenching.

After she spent the morning sightseeing with him, they later shared an inexpensive lunch at a hotel coffee shop. From there they walked around breathing in the sights and sounds of Bangkok until the sweltering heat drove them in search of refreshment again.

'No wonder we're hot!' Kevin exclaimed as they entered the beautifully welcoming air-conditioned confines of a large department store called Sogo. 'We must have walked miles!'

'You're not fit!' Delfi ribbed him.

'For that I'll treat you to a pizza,' he grandly offered.

'You couldn't!' she exclaimed, while refusing his offer, incredulous at his appetite after what he'd put away at lunchtime.

'I'm a growing lad!' he protested, but laughed, and as they found a café within the building and he ordered a pizza Delfi decided that her easy-to-get-along-with companion, as well as being a growing lad, was a very nice lad too. She sincerely hoped that all his problems with regard to his studies would resolve themselves to his benefit.

Delfi found that talking over all sorts of matters that were of no importance with Kevin helped to amicably speed her day. In any event, many were the times when just chatting to him kept thoughts of Hugh, or her sister, or even Boden McLaine, at bay.

That being so, she had no wish to return to the hotel and to the solitude of the four walls of her room in a hurry. Eventually, however, she and Kevin left the comfortable confines of the air-conditioning and went outside to the heat, noise and crowded thoroughfares of Bangkok. 'Where to?' Kevin asked, seeming keen to prolong their day.

But Delfi suddenly experienced a feeling of restlessness, and even though there was still no need to hurry back she nevertheless glanced at her watch. 'It's five o'clock,' she told him, 'I think I'll go back to the hotel.'

'Shall we try a *tuk-tuk*?' he suggested, falling in without complication with whatever she said, as the driver of a small, open-sided, three-wheeled taxi manoeuvred out of the congested traffic to where they stood.

'I'm game if you are,' she replied, and didn't have time to spare to feel restless or to think about anything but hanging on as, aboard the *tuk-tuk*, they raced at bone-rattling speed over every bump in the road.

'Strewth!' Kevin exclaimed when, shaken, they arrived at their destination. And having paid the driver off they were still animatedly discussing the experience when they entered the spacious foyer of the hotel. 'I was hoping to get a few shots of street scenes, but no chance,' he laughed. And as Delfi shared his laughter, 'I swear that driver took every corner on one wheel,' he added

'Did you see——?' Delfi began, laughter still curving her lovely mouth when suddenly, as they neared the reception desk, a tall fair-haired man turned around—and her voice froze in her throat. Boden McLaine had spotted her at once—and from his grim expression, she saw that he did not look very pleased about something. 'Oh— er—here's—er—my employer.' She changed what she had been about to say, having already told Kevin that she had a job she would soon be starting. Then, while refusing to be put down by any black look McLaine threw her—and since he was now blocking her path to the desk—she did the only thing she could. 'Good evening, Mr McLaine,' she greeted him, and not waiting for any reply she launched into cool introductions. 'This is Kevin Carroll, from Devizes. Kevin, Mr McLaine, my—temporary boss.'

It would not have surprised her had Boden McLaine totally ignored the hand which Kevin shot out. But she saw she had to give him top marks for manners, even though it seemed that something had upset him. He's probably had a bad day at the exhibition, she decided as he shook hands with Kevin and enquired if he was staying in this hotel too.

'Only for another few days, then I'm moving on to Malaysia,' Kevin replied with his open smile. And turning to Delfi, 'If you're free tomorrow, Delfi, we could——'

'I'm afraid I've other plans for Delfi, for tomorrow,'
Boden McLaine cut in pleasantly, and while Kevin transferred his respectful gaze to him Delfi, not quite able to
believe her ears at the pleasantness of his tone, stared
at him. She was still staring at him, more because when
she'd thought she'd be Miss Washington to him forever-
more he had actually called her by the more friendly
version of her first name than from surprise that, by the
sound of it, she would be working tomorrow, when he
added, still in that same pleasant tone, 'We'll discuss it
over dinner,' and with an affable nod to Kevin strolled
off.

Delfi was still trying to equate the glowering man she
had first seen with the pleasant man who had just left
them as she and Kevin claimed their room keys.

'If you do happen to have a free day before I leave,
perhaps you'll leave a message or phone my room,' Kevin
suggested hopefully as they went up in the lift together.

'I will,' Delfi promised, and had time only in which
to exchange quick mutual thanks for the other's company
when the lift stopped at her floor. 'Bye.' She smiled, and
as the lift doors closed she turned and went along to her
room.

Kevin Carroll had gone from her mind by the time
she'd had a refreshing shower and stood unpacking a
few more of her belongings from her suitcase. Boden
McLaine had not said at what time they would dine, but
since he'd suggested—no, instructed—that they'd dine
at eight the previous evening she reckoned that eight
would be about the time that they would eat tonight.

Thoughts of home penetrated as she sorted through
to select something to wear to dinner. But as dark clouds
of unhappiness threatened, Delfi valiantly battled to keep
home thoughts away. She had been right to leave
England, she endorsed yet again. She must not give in

to sickness of heart and return. This way, no matter how painful, was the only way.

At ten to eight Delfi had had sufficient of the four walls of her room as to want to leave them. In a dress of deep blue which enhanced the violet of her eyes and the fairness of her skin and hair, she moved with unconscious grace towards the lifts.

She was in sombre mood as the lift carried her downwards, but tried to appear serene and composed and as if everything were wonderful with her world. She stepped from the lift and walked a few paces to her right and was in the spacious lounge area that abounded with softly padded chairs and settees when suddenly she spotted the tall and athletic shape of Boden McLaine coming towards her.

She thought for one moment that she glimpsed a hint of admiration in his glance as he drew near, but when he had halted in front of her all that she could see in his look was the coolness she was used to seeing.

Wordlessly he touched her elbow to direct her in the way they would go, but as they fell into step he let go his hold, and she liked it that way. The mood she found herself in, she didn't want human touch. They had entered the same dining-room they had used the previous evening when it dawned on her that while she did not want human touch she must want human contact of some sort, or why had she left her room?

That was easily explained, she realised, when an attentive head waiter had shown them to the secluded table they had dined at the previous evening and seen them seated; she needed human contact, if only to get thoughts of England and her near treachery to dear Raina out of her head. She——

'Are things that bad?'

'Wh...' Delfi came to with a start, and realised then at Boden McLaine's harshly asked question that this sharp-eyed man didn't miss much. 'Oh, sorry,' she added lightly, having more pride than to want him to know any of what was paining her, 'I was miles away.' With that, she took refuge in the menu and hoped to turn her temporary employer's thoughts away from any speculations he might or might not be making about her. 'Am I going to come to grief if I sample the *yam nuea*, would you say?'

For several moments he favoured her with a tough, no-nonsense kind of look, then, 'You're learning fast,' he grunted in reference to the way she had gone her own way and ordered a dish that was too hotly spiced for her palate the evening before. 'You'll be fine with that,' he conceded.

Delfi did not thank him. She was not, in point of fact, very taken with him just then. Which was why she tucked into her first course with barely another word coming from her. In fact she was nearly through her *yam nuea*, which turned out to be charcoal-grilled beef marinaded with chillies and lime, and on a bed of rice—and which was quite tasty—before she so much as looked at him again.

To her surprise, though, when she did look at him she found that he had his eyes on her, and for all she could tell could have been staring at her semi-bent head for some minutes. 'Er—this is delicious.' She trotted out the first thing that came to her.

He ignored her comment and, having finished his main course, waited the minute or two for her to finish hers then, leaning back in his chair, he reached into the inside pocket of his jacket and extracted a bulky envelope. 'Put this in your bag,' he coolly instructed.

Without thought, she took the envelope from him. 'What is it?' she asked, and as the envelope flap was loose she pulled it back to see that it contained a goodly sum of money—all sterling. With wide eyes her glance shot to him.

'It's the sum we agreed,' he answered. 'If you wish the cashier here will change it into baht for you.'

Suddenly light dawned. McLaine had this morning told her how much he intended to pay her. She had never imagined, though, that he intended to pay her in advance. She said as much.

'I sort of rather expected to be paid at the end of the job rather than before,' she told him, and, while their table was so secluded that no one could see what was going on, she obeyed his earlier instruction and put the money away in her bag.

He shrugged, then announced, 'Even though I doubt there'll be any opportunity for you to spend very much where we're going, it struck me that a month's a long time to be without funds.'

Delfi supposed that she'd only got herself to blame that he thought she was a pauper. Hadn't she told him herself that she could only afford one night in this hotel? There was not a lot she could say in answer to him, she realised. So, 'Thank you,' she said solemnly, and as the waiter came and cleared away and took their orders for pudding she spent a few quiet minutes wishing she were back in her room, then being glad that she wasn't and then facing squarely the fact that, at that precise moment, she didn't know just where the dickens she was.

The gâteau she had ordered was in front of her, and she was just daintily tucking in to her second spoonful when Boden McLaine startled her by suddenly asking, 'Is that how you're usually called—Delfi?'

She swallowed her second spoonful of gâteau then found, as an imp of mischief stirred, that there was no joy to be found in being continually down about things which one had no control over. 'It has to be better than Adelfia, wouldn't you agree?' she answered, her mouth starting to pick up at the corners in a smile.

She saw McLaine's glance go to her mouth, but by no chance was a smile going to make an appearance on his cold exterior, she realised. For, far from smiling, he looked more forbidding than ever. 'Do you think you're being wise?' he grated.

'Wise?' she queried.

Her smile had fast gone into hiding when, his look arctic, he harshly snarled, 'I'd have thought that after having been singed by one man you'd have more sense than to so quickly allow yourself to be picked up by another.'

For all of three seconds, Delfi thought he must be referring to the love she had run away from. Then as intelligence took over from emotion she realised that he couldn't possibly know about Hugh and how she felt more scalded than singed on his account. But, having worked out that he must mean Mel Dalloway, she did not care at all for his implication that Kevin Carroll had then 'picked her up'—they were just two English people in a foreign land who'd joined forces for the day, that was all.

Somehow, she managed to hang on to her temper. Then, 'Picked up?' she queried, as she pretended that she hadn't a clue what he was talking about. 'Oh!' she exclaimed then, as if what he was alluding to had just come to her. '*You*, do you mean?' she asked, all huge-eyed and innocent.

'You know damn well I don't mean me!' Boden McLaine blazed, explosively.

'Oh,' she murmured in sham surprise. Then suddenly, while he glared a fuming, hostile glare at her, she smiled a delicious smile. 'I think I'll turn in now,' she told him sweetly, and not certain that he wouldn't suddenly break into a bellow of rage, as looked likely, she grabbed up her bag and did a swift retreat.

Delfi was still smiling as she entered her room. Indeed, she was inwardly chuckling as she tossed her bag to the bed and went over to the window. She stared out into the darkness at the illuminated craft on the river, and could only wonder that, when she had been in most heavy spirits when she'd left her room earlier, she should suddenly be feeling so good inside.

When later she undressed and got into bed, Delfi was still feeling better inside than she had—though she could hardly believe that her small clash of swords with Boden McLaine was responsible. It had to be that though, she realised, and just then realised something else—McLaine had said that he'd discuss with her over dinner his plans for tomorrow. Oh, lord, she thought as she remembered the way she'd sailed out of the dining-room, she'd got out of there before he had discussed anything with her to do with business. She closed her eyes knowing that she'd have to be down to breakfast at the same time as this morning—she'd better get some sleep; it could be a busy, busy day tomorrow.

CHAPTER FOUR

TRUE to her plan, Delfi was up early the following morning, and down to breakfast a few minutes earlier than the previous morning. Boden McLaine, she discovered, was already there.

It was she, this time, who went over to his table. 'Good morning, Mr McLaine,' she greeted him pleasantly, and as he automatically made to rise she smiled, reserved a place at his table by dropping that morning's edition of the *Nation* on to a spare chair and turned about to go to the self-service area.

McLaine, she silently acknowledged as she helped herself to orange juice, had been quite something in a business suit. Today, though, he had exchanged business attire for casual garb—she was hard put to it to decide which became him more. He certainly looked more relaxed today in his sports shirt and casual trousers, she decided, then suddenly stopped mid-thought. Grief! As if it mattered a jot!

Delfi returned to Boden McLaine's table having realised that seeing her temporary employer dressed as if he intended to have a day off must have thrown her. She knew for sure—since he'd got 'plans' for her for that day—that they'd both be working. She took her place opposite him concluding that, since it was so very hot outside—even with the most efficient air-conditioning inside—he must have taken against wearing a business suit, no matter how lightweight.

Seated opposite him she took a sip of her orange juice. As yet, Boden McLaine had addressed not one syllable to her. Briefly, she wondered if he was brooding about something, and then decided that there was only one way to find out.

'Am I to go with you to the exhibition today?' she asked for openers, and looked directly at him to observe that he was flicking an all-assessing glance over her neat, cool and tailored dress which she hoped, along with her two-and-a-half-inch-heeled shoes, was the epitome of what today's efficient secretary was wearing. Surprise, tremendous surprise awaited her, however, when, transferring his glance to her face, he deigned to reply.

'I'm not going to the exhibition today,' he divulged coolly.

'You're—not?' she questioned, her eyes riveted to the aloof blue-green of his.

'I've staff there who can cope quite well without me,' he informed her, and after a moment or two, 'I've decided to take the day off and leave them to it.'

'But ... but ...' Swiftly Delfi got her cool self together to remind him, 'You said, yesterday evening, that you'd plans for me today.'

'Had you last night stayed around for long enough, you might have heard what they were,' he in turn reminded her. She'd see him hang before she'd apologise for that, she thought, starting to get disgruntled by his manner. 'Today I'm minded to take a look at some Thai culture.'

'Thai culture?' she repeated uncertainly, wondering what the deuce Thai culture had to do with her secretarial skills.

'Apropos the research I've to do for my father, it seemed an idea to try to get a feel of the Thai background before I start the work in earnest,' he replied airily, and added, with an indifferent shrug, 'It occurred to me that you might feel better equipped if you did the same.'

Delfi took another sip of her orange juice. She couldn't argue with that, she realised. 'You're the boss,' she told him.

'That's true,' he replied, and for the rest of the meal ignored her while he fed the inner man.

Delfi was sorely tempted by then to take the *Nation* out of its plastic wrapper and scan through the situations vacant columns just to let him know that if there was a better job going than the one he offered she'd jolly well take it. There were two things against that though. The one, that she had last night scrutinised every inch of yesterday's situations vacant, and had not seen one which, with her lack of the languages necessary, she was qualified for. She had no wish to invite more of McLaine's lofty looks if, not forgetting her lack of a work permit, there was nothing suitable in the paper today too. She could not forget, either, that last night McLaine had generously paid her in advance for a month's work. In accepting his money, she realised, she had accepted the job.

By the time she left the restaurant with him, she had swung round from being not a little fed up with him to wonder what she was thinking of. She was glad to accept his offer of a job—for goodness' sake, without it she'd be in a real spot.

'I'll see you here in ten minutes,' he paused to instruct as they reached the lifts.

'Ten minutes it is, Mr McLaine,' she answered efficiently, and pressed the lift call button, then saw that just as he had seemed about to go striding on he had hesitated.

'Er—since I'm having a day off—make it Boden,' he suggested—and left her staring after him.

Ten minutes was not a long time. Delfi dived into her room and, as swiftly, dived into her suitcase. Somewhere, she had a pair of trousers. Had she not marched out of the dining-room the way she had last night, she'd have learned sufficient to know that today was a day for casual attire. She remembered Boden McLaine's cool eyes on her tailored dress—he was trying to tell her something.

Three minutes later the tailored dress was on her bed and Delfi was pulling on a smart pair of equally tailored white trousers. She teamed them with the only thing resembling a loose shirt she had with her, found some sandals and had time only to hang her dress on a hanger, then she was leaving her room.

Only then, as she went down in the lift, did she have chance to dwell on the fact that, albeit seemingly reluctantly, McLaine had invited her to use his first name.

'Ah—there you are!' he greeted her when she went up to him and, not commenting on the fact that she had changed out of her tailored dress—but that fact noted, she was sure—he suddenly smiled. Just as suddenly, Delfi felt warmed inside. 'I've a car waiting,' he said. Delfi too was smiling as she went with him to the chauffeur-driven limousine.

She had no clue to where exactly they were going when, having finally cleared the mass of Bangkok's traffic, they motored out of the area and into the countryside.

She found everything of enormous interest, and shortly after they passed a laden-to-capacity lorryload of coconuts they came to a coconut plantation. But there was other industry too, including a prawn farm and, when she enquired about the many seemingly barren fields, she discovered that they were salt fields. This knowledge preoccupied her for some time as she realised that the fields must first be flooded with salt water, and then, presumably, allowed to dry out.

A couple of hours after they left Bangkok, the chauffeur pulled into a jetty. 'I'm reliably informed that no visit to Thailand is complete without a visit to a floating market,' Boden informed her.

'Er—it sounds exciting,' Delfi volunteered, with no idea of what went on at a floating market.

Half an hour later she did have more idea, but was more impressed by the actual getting there than the market itself. She was glad though that she'd changed into trousers when a quite basic sharp-ended motorised narrow boat arrived, and her temporary employer helped her down into it. No sooner had he come and sat beside her than the engine sprang into noisy life, and they were off down what seemed to her to be a town on stilts, with streets that were a fretwork of canals.

She gathered, when they made a little detour, that they must be travelling up the main street. There were houses on either side of the waterway with walkways like pavements from home to home. Occasionally a punt or similar craft would pass going the other way, sometimes with children, plainly more than at home on the water, its only occupants.

As they approached a landing-stage, they came across many other open boats, with women wearing large basketweave, lampshade-shape hats ferrying cargo ranging from bananas, pineapples, vegetables and flowers to tinned goods.

The market itself was reached by steps from the landing-stage, and was a busy commercial proposition. They did not spend long in looking round the market, and Delfi, who by then had no clue to where in the world they were except Thailand, went where her escort led when they walked away from the waterway area. It could not have been longer than five minutes later that they came to where their chauffeur and limousine were waiting for them.

Delfi had rather gathered that Boden McLaine had never been to Thailand before. She got into the car realising that he nevertheless seemed to know his way around wherever he was. Unerringly he had led the way to where the chauffeur had brought the vehicle round to meet them.

'I quite enjoyed that,' she saw no harm in letting Boden know.

'You like the water?' he questioned perfectly amicably.

'I think I must!'

'That's as well,' he commented drily, and when she looked questioningly, 'We're lunching by a lake,' he informed her.

It was little short of idyllic by the lake. After the noise of the power-driven boat, and the activity at the market, Delfi equally enjoyed just sitting watching the calm clear waters.

There seemed to be any number of curries on the lunchtime menu, and Delfi was very much drawn to *gaeng keo warn gai*, which was a green chicken curry, but she'd had a brush with highly spiced Thai food before, and discretion won the day.

'I think I'll have the *pad preow wan goong*,' she determinedly got her tongue round the Thai pronunciation to inform Boden.

'You're sure?' he enquired, and she was suddenly certain that there was a hint of devilment in his eyes.

Her lips twitched. 'I'm sure,' she said sedately, and lest she should burst out laughing she suddenly found the tablecloth of immense interest.

Her sweet and sour prawns were served on a bed of rice, and were quite delicious, and, oddly, conversation did not seem necessary as between forkfuls she would every now and then look out to the lake and find she was feeling quite tranquil herself.

After the meal they walked through some gardens, and from there they walked on, where she discovered many other people were heading in the same direction.

'What do you know that I don't?' she felt compelled to ask.

She then discovered that Boden McLaine did have a sense of humour when, with amusement most definitely tugging at his firm but well-shaped mouth, he murmured, 'Quite a bit and then some, by all accounts,' but answered what he must have known all along was a more specific question, 'In the hope that it hasn't strayed too far from authenticity, we're taking in a Thai cultural show.'

Delfi found yet more enjoyment when in the crowded circular theatre she sat beside him looking down into the centre arena. Somewhere to her right music—bells, xylophone, flute and drums—began to play, and as dancers filed into the circle below Delfi in no time was lost.

By the end of the performance she owned that her knowledge of Thai culture was a degree or two improved. 'Did you "quite" enjoy that too?' Boden queried, and when as early ago as that morning she would have found cause to be disgruntled by his manner, she decided that he was teasing and not sarcastic.

'Quite,' she replied, and walked to the car with him amicably discussing the merits and otherwise of the show which, in the main, had been quite charming.

With her head full of the show, she sat quietly in the car as it started its journey back to Bangkok. Aside from the gorgeous costumes of the most elegant and graceful dancers, there had also been a narrated procession connected with Buddhist monks. It was from the narration that Delfi learned that all Thai men became ordained as monks for a short time in their lives when after the novice period they wore saffron-coloured robes and studied the precepts of Buddhism before leaving to take up family life and responsibilities. There had been a three-round exhibition of Thai boxing too, but with music being played in the background, and, what with the hands, elbows, knees and *feet* of the boxers flying fast and furiously, it had seemed more amusing than pugilistic. More dancing had followed, then a presentation of a Thai wedding.

Unconsciously Delfi sighed, Hugh Renshaw there in her head as she recalled how after the ceremony the couple had moved to an altar to say prayers together, and then moved from the altar to receive blessings from relatives and friends. To signify unity the happy couple had been linked together by a circle of cord stretching from the woman's head to the man's. Then to wish them everlasting happiness, relatives and friends had poured water over the couple's hands to the earth below.

Delfi's thoughts moved on, and she was deep in Hugh Renshaw territory, knowing that it would kill her to be bridesmaid at her sister's wedding as had been mooted. She bit her lip in anguish and was battling hard to push away thoughts of Hugh and how, because of Raina, she could never be his wife, when she was rudely shaken out of her thoughts.

'What goes on in your head?' Boden McLaine suddenly demanded—just as if he had every right to know!

'Wh...' she began, noting that his curt way of speaking to her was back, and before the basic antagonism he aroused in her began to stir. That antagonism had arrived in full measure though when she flew, 'It hasn't anything to do with you!'

'It has if I'm going to have to put up with you sobbing and sighing all over the place when we go up north!' he told her in no uncertain terms.

'Sobbing and sighing!' she exclaimed, and hotly refuting any such suggestion, 'I was doing nothing of the sort!' she flared. Though, when the look he tossed her virtually called her a liar, she, because she'd no idea in her head of any sound she might have made when she'd been thinking sad thoughts of Hugh, quickly found an excuse that would cover any expression of sadness she might have worn. 'As a matter of fact,' she went on tartly, 'I was thinking of that Thai wedding ceremony we watched. In case you haven't heard,' she added stiffly, 'all women go moist-eyed at weddings!' There, she thought crossly, staring at him coldly, make a meal out of that! She hated him—when he did.

'Rot!' he scorned, her cold looks not bothering him one iota. Then as a shrewd and annoyed look came to his eyes, 'You were thinking of weddings though,' and followed up quickly, 'Your own? Have you run away from England rather than marry some man you were engaged to?' he demanded. 'Have you——?'

'*No, I have not!*' she exploded, then belatedly realised that her tone was too vehement, just as though he'd hit a nerve. 'For your information,' she informed him more quietly, 'I have never been engaged.'

'But you wanted to be,' he quickly sifted through what she'd said. 'Only he didn't want to marry you.' He frowned then, as though to him that didn't seem quite right. 'Ah!' he in a flash worked out, clearly having done some rapid thinking. 'It wasn't that he didn't want to marry you, but couldn't. He isn't free—he's already married——'

But Delfi had had enough. 'Stop right there!' burst from her as her fury got the better of her. 'Whether there's some man in my life or there isn't is nothing to do with the job you've hired me to do!'

'It has if you fall down on the job while mooning over your lost love!' he barked.

'Do you want your money back?' she erupted.

'You've more emotion than brains—you're broke, remember?' he snarled, his chin jutting up at a warning angle.

Delfi could have done without the reminder—it served to temper her fury, and she felt better able to cope with the all-seeing brute whom she happened to be employed by when she was furious. Clamping her lips tightly together, she turned her head and stared out of the window.

She had not opened them again when the limousine drew up outside their hotel. She walked to the desk and asked a male receptionist for her room key. Fate being what it was, the pretty female receptionist who went on the same errand for Boden McLaine returned with his key first.

He thanked her pleasantly, but his pleasant manner had disappeared when, turning to Delfi—every bit as though he'd read her mind, 'Don't stay sulking in your room. Join me for dinner,' he commanded toughly.

'Is that an order?' she asked, cold-eyed and hating.

'Believe it,' he snarled.

Delfi was not liking Boden McLaine any better when on Saturday morning she stared from the windows in her room, with her luggage packed. Shortly they would leave for the airport; shortly, they would fly to some place in the north called Chiang Mai. Then, she supposed, she would start work.

She had dined with him last night and the night before, and, although she'd discovered that he had innate good manners and never made her feel awkward or uncomfortable when there was anyone else about, he had not stirred himself overmuch to talk to her when there was not. Since she was far from fussed about speaking to him either unless she had to, she, on Thursday night, had given her attention to a thunderstorm going on outside. It was a localised storm, she had noted as she looked out, and she had in truth been fascinated for quite some minutes to see how, just as though the storm were contained in one dark cloud, lightning within that cloud lit up that cloud only.

On Friday, when again 'ordered' to dine with the man she loved to hate, they again had had little to say to each other. Though it was that evening that she'd learned that, instead of Boden McLaine's putting in some time at the exhibition the next day, he had no such intention.

Apparently a traditional Thai festival called Loy Krathong was to be celebrated on Saturday and Sunday, marking the night of the full moon of the twelve lunar months when the rivers and canals in Thailand would be at their highest. Beautifully constructed 'Krathong' made of banana leaves and flowers were placed in the water by the Thai people to honour the water spirits and to carry away their sins. A lighted candle was placed in the Krathong and it was said that if the candle stayed lit wishes would be fulfilled.

'Will we be here for the firework display tomorrow night?' Delfi forgot that she hadn't anything she wanted to say to him as, her thoughts following on, the question had slipped out.

'Much as I hate to deprive you of such innocent pleasure,' he returned coldly, seemingly having quite easily hopped on to her wavelength about Loy Krathong, 'we're leaving in the morning.'

Delfi looked hostilely into Boden McLaine's cold blue-green eyes and fought with the impulse to up-end her pudding plate over his head. Having conquered that impulse, she then fought another which would have seen her getting up and leaving.

A couple of days ago she would have walked out, she knew. But she was learning, so she stayed where she was and, with more effort than he would ever know about, searched hard and found a pleasant note to tell him, 'I hope I never get so sated that I miss out on the simple things in life.' And, with more control arriving all the time, instead of just getting up and marching away from him, since fireworks had featured in the conversation, 'If you'll excuse me,' she said sweetly, 'I think I'll touch the blue paper and retire.'

He rose with her, but as her hostile glance clashed with the aggression in his she just knew that he wasn't going to let her get away with saying anything she felt like saying so easily. 'I should,' he drawled, his tone vastly at odds with the ice in his eyes. 'You haven't yet recovered from having your fingers burned once before, have you?'

Swine, Delfi had dubbed him as she marched angrily back to her room. She'd gone to bed still thinking him a swine, and had not seen any reason to change her opinion this morning when, breakfastless, she waited for him to contact her. She'd be damned if she'd share breakfast with him. He knew where she was; if he wanted her he could jolly well get in touch.

Boden McLaine did not contact her direct, but made it known that they were about to leave by sending a porter up to her room for her luggage. Delfi stayed behind to take a last checking look round her room. Then, certain she had left nothing behind, she muttered, 'Goodbye, Bangkok; hello, Chiang Mai,' and left her room knowing that what with one thing and another the next month up in Chiang Mai was going to be the longest month of her life.

The four-hundred-odd-mile flight to Chiang Mai took an hour—it had taken as long again for them to drive out of Bangkok to the airport. But both journeys were uneventful. Chiang Mai, she'd learned from a map, was quite a way up in the north, was the second-largest city in Thailand and was nicknamed the Rose of the North.

They went by taxi to a smart hotel, where a porter came forward to take their luggage, and Boden escorted her inside. 'I expect you'd like some lunch,' he said, turning to her midway through the formalities of booking them in.

If that was a knock because she'd missed breakfast Delfi chose to ignore it. She hadn't felt like anything to eat on the plane either, but suddenly she was feeling next door to starving. 'If it's not too late,' she replied, checking her watch to see that it was way past lunchtime.

Naturally, since in her opinion it was unthinkable that McLaine should go hungry, the gently smiling pretty receptionist, when asked about food, looked as if ready to cook a meal herself for him if need be. It didn't come to that, but she called someone over to take them to the dining-room.

'I've a guest dining with us this evening,' Boden McLaine let up on hostilities to inform her as she ended her meal of meat, nuts and rice.

A most peculiar sensation chose that moment to hit her in the pit of the stomach, and Delfi raised startled eyes to his. Somehow, though of course it wasn't in the least important, she had rather thought that it would be just she and Boden in Chiang Mai. That he clearly had some female there he'd arranged to see was a bit of a surprise. It explained though why he'd cut the exhibition today—the lady must be of some importance to him!

'You want me to stay out of the way?' Delfi enquired.

'What the devil are you talking about?' he grated, back to being his pleasant best.

'I thought . . . I meant . . . If you've a lady friend here, then——'

'Unlike you, Miss Washington,' he cut her off shortly, 'I'm able to handle my "affairs of the heart" without any problems,' and while her hackles instantly started to rise he reiterated, 'I said I've a guest dining with *us*.' While she mutinied and did not miss the implication that were he dining with a lady friend then he most definitely would not include her, he continued, 'Dr Phothiat is an anthropologist friend of my father. He's been good enough to say he'll come and fill me in on anything I wish to know.'

Wishing at that point that somebody would fill McLaine in permanently, and as her insides started to settle down again, she realised that she must in her hunger have eaten her meat, nuts and rice too quickly. 'Do you want me to bring a notepad?' she enquired.

'That shouldn't be necessary,' he replied, then his sharp glance raked her face. 'You look tired!' he stated curtly. 'Are you sleeping all right?'

Had she thought he was concerned—more than that, he didn't want her to go to sleep on the job— Delfi might have smiled and lied that she was clocking up a full eight hours every night. But, since she knew that his only worry was that she might not be bright-eyed and bushy-tailed when he started cracking the whip, she was feeling just perverse enough not to want to lie.

'Perhaps, if there's nothing you want me for, I'll catch up on some sleep this afternoon,' she replied.

'I hope he's worth it!' he grunted, and Delfi hated him—and his insight—afresh. He knew, since it wasn't him she was losing sleep over, that thoughts of the man she'd run from in England were giving her the midnight horrors.

Not that it was only thoughts of Hugh Renshaw that started to get to her in the small waking hours, Delfi recalled as she went and found her room. Her head was such a jumble of thoughts when at any odd hour in the night she would wake and find it impossible to get to sleep again. Thoughts of Raina, and the near nervous breakdown she had suffered when her first fiancé had jilted her, haunted her. Guilt and shame were then Delfi's companions that she had ever, so willingly, so entirely without thought, gone into Hugh Renshaw's arms.

Delfi was not liking Boden McLaine any better when, dressed in a smart pale green dress of delicate silk, she left her room that evening. She had not slept at all but, as more guilt and shame had visited her, she had again swung round to be grateful to the taciturn brute McLaine that he was doing her one very big favour by employing her for a whole month.

She stepped out of the lift and made for the lounge area where she thought she'd wait, knowing that she didn't have to like McLaine. She'd do a good job for him, nevertheless, she asserted; she owed him that much.

Her decision to wait in the lounge for him was negated when, treading into that thickly carpeted area, she saw that he was already there. So too, if she was not mistaken, looking quite small beside the height and breadth of Boden's shoulders, was his guest.

'I'm sorry if I'm late,' she apologised at once as both men got to their feet as she went over to them.

'Not at all,' the small dark-haired Thai man smiled charmingly, 'I am very early. Is that not so, Boden?' he enquired of the tall fair-haired man.

Boden McLaine was looking cool, confident and relaxed, Delfi observed when, with his glance skimming over her from the top of her silver-blonde hair and over her pale green dress that elegantly suited her to the tip of her classically clad feet, he performed the introductions. 'Delfi has agreed to help me in this work I'm to do for my father,' he added easily.

'You have been married long?' Dr Phothiat smilingly asked.

Delfi shot Dr Phothiat a startled glance. Then, as she realised that he must think that she and Boden were married, she started to correct that mistake without delay. Unfortunately Boden McLaine clearly didn't like the idea of their being paired together any better than she did, and began at the same time to put his own correction in. Which meant she only got as far as 'Oh—we're not... when her voice became buried under his.

'Marriage is not a step I've ever contemplated,' he told Dr Phothiat pleasantly.

'Oh—I see,' Dr Phothiat replied, but Delfi was certain that he jolly well didn't. And that made her angry, not at the anthropologist, but at Boden McLaine.

The way she saw it, as she sent him a glare of barely masked dislike, he was making it sound every bit as though he'd never contemplated marriage because he'd no need to, because she—was his mistress! Delfi at once forgot about any feelings of gratitude, and Boden McLaine was back to being a swine in her book when she attempted to set the record straight.

'Actually, Dr Phothiat,' she smiled, 'I'm Boden's secretary.' Why had she called McLaine by his first name? She couldn't get over it—it was the first time she had!

Delfi was staring at his guest, whom she'd just attempted to set straight, feeling a good deal dumbstruck at how friendly she'd sounded to that monster she was going to work for, when Dr Phothiat, in common with all Thais she'd had dealings with, proved he was a man full of smiles.

'Oh, yes,' he beamed, and Delfi gave up. Quite plainly, he didn't believe a word of it, but was much too polite to ever dream of saying so.

The three of them went in to dinner, and Delfi realised that if Dr Phothiat was Boden's guest then, since Boden was her employer, she must regard Dr Phothiat as her guest too.

There were many times, however, as the meal progressed when she was required to do nothing more than tune in and listen. Though to start with the discussion between the two men was not entirely about the work that Boden had undertaken to do on his father's behalf.

'How is Teresa? She is well?' Dr Phothiat asked as they started on their first course.

Oddly Delfi, who had eaten nothing since her late lunch, again felt that peculiar sensation hit the pit of her stomach that she had then. She dismissed it and concentrated on hearing Boden's reply to how some woman friend—whom he must know well for Dr Phothiat to have knowledge of her—was.

'My father's married to Gina now,' Boden answered his question, leaving Delfi to guess that Teresa must be his father's second wife.

Dr Phothiat's next question seemed to confirm it. 'Oh, so it is one of *Gina's* children who had the accident and is the reason why your father cannot be here,' he worked out after a moment. Then he smiled, a warm broad smile, and it was clear that he thought a lot of Boden's father.

'One day perhaps, when I see my old friend again, I may meet the third Mrs McLaine.'

From there talk drifted on to Boden being there to do what research he could on his father's behalf. Delfi tucked daintily into her second course and listened with interest. Though it wasn't too long before she started to feel a prickle of apprehension at what she was hearing. She had, over the last few hours—ridiculously, she now realised—somehow grown to the idea that Boden's research would be done in the area near to where they were. Chiang Mai, according to the map, was in the distant north, so, from what she'd so far taken in about the hill tribes of the Kariang and Meo being near to Chiang Mai, it hadn't seemed such a ridiculous assumption. But the Kariang and Meo people could not be the tribes Boden was interested in, because here was Dr Phothiat questioning him about when did they propose to fly on up to Chiang Rai—a place yet further north by all accounts!

'I'd like to get on as soon as possible in the morning. I've a flight booked,' Boden answered.

'Chiang Rai?' Delfi couldn't hold back the query.

'It's in the northernmost province of my country,' Dr Phothiat smilingly replied, and turned to Boden to suggest, 'A Land Rover will be your best form of transport from there. With good fortune,' he looked her way to smile again, 'there should be few times that you will have to get out and push.'

'Push!' she exclaimed, her rose-coloured glasses hitting the ground with a bump as the word 'primitive' shot into her head. 'Is the—er—road a bit—er—pot-holey?'

Her spirits took a rapid nosedive, and she wasn't sure that she didn't actually lose some of her colour when Dr Phothiat, still smiling his sunny smile, happily told her that there was no road as she knew roads, but a dirt clearing. 'In places,' he continued cheerfully, 'you'll find it will be little more than a path through the jungle.'

Jungle! Good heavens! Delfi swallowed hard as she grappled with the nightmarish thought that 'primitive' might not begin to describe it! Under the cover of Boden and Dr Phothiat getting down to more earnest discussion, she did what she could to get herself back together. But, by the time the dessert stage had been reached, it had alarmingly dawned on her that with regard to the clothes she had with her she was hopelessly inadequately equipped!

Coffee had been served when Delfi, while aware that she had packed only smart clothes, experienced a desperate urge to return to her room to see if anything in her wardrobe would suit the bill for what looked like a month in—she swallowed—the jungle. Even while she knew that, because there was only so much one could bring, she had opted to leave her casual clothes at home, she just could not wait to go and check.

'Anything wrong, Delfi?' Boden McLaine's suddenly, if coolly, addressing her brought her to an awareness that there was little he missed.

'Nothing at all,' she lightly denied, but, dinner virtually over, she found a pleasant smile for both him and the doctor, and added, 'Tomorrow sounds like being a busy day. If you'll excuse me, I think I'll have an early night.'

Having said her goodbyes to Dr Phothiat, Delfi left the dining-room and made for the lifts. Boden McLaine had seemed not to care one way or the other whether she stayed or went. Though from the crusty look he tossed her she knew that he wasn't believing in any 'I think I'll have an early night' excuse. Not when, since he knew that she wasn't sleeping well, he would also know that there was little point in her going to bed early.

Once she was in her room Delfi forgot all about Boden McLaine and began straight away to sort through her clothes. Fifteen minutes later the sum total of what she considered to be suitable apparel was laid out on her bed. It did not amount to much. At a push, and stretching the bounds of jungle fashion to extremes, she had one pair of tailored trousers, one shirt, a silk blouse and a pair of flimsy sandals.

Another five minutes went by during which time Delfi despaired that even if her sandals stayed the course, which was doubtful, then how in creation was she going to manage with the rest of her gear?

When the whimsical thought arrived that perhaps she could stay in bed while her clothes were washed and dried, Delfi thought it was time to take a shower and get ready for bed. She was under the shower when an even worse thought struck: always supposing—since she had no idea how deep into the jungle they were going—that she had a bed at all!

Half an hour later Delfi was sitting up in her bed. Sleep was miles away as her head spun with thoughts of her limited wardrobe and of what she had committed herself to. Since it was still so vitally important that she did not return home, however, to go with Boden McLaine was, she accepted, her only option.

She was just starting to thaw a little about him, acknowledging once again that without his offer of paid employment she'd have been in something of a pickle, when a sharp rap sounded on her door. Getting out of bed she pulled a robe around her and went to answer it—and immediately any thawing in her froze over.

'Yes?' she asked the tall McLaine, thoroughly annoyed with him suddenly that his visit an hour after she'd left him with the stated intention to have an early night just confirmed that he knew she wouldn't be asleep. Not only that, but with him looking loftily down on her she felt at a distinct disadvantage in her night clothes and with not a scrap of make-up on.

'So—what's wrong?' he questioned curtly.

Grief—did he *never* give up? 'I said nothing was wrong!' she reiterated sharply—and immediately saw that he didn't take kindly to being fed the same lie twice.

'You physically blanched when Dr Phothiat hinted that we were heading into the jungle!' he rounded on her curtly, and went on to aggressively accuse, 'You're afraid of anything that might resemble hard toil. You—with your dainty hands—are terrified you might——'

'No, I'm not!' she exploded in a fury that seemed to surprise him as much as it surprised her. His eyes were fixed on the angry light in hers anyhow when, holding down any further accusations he might have, he waited for her to go on. 'I'm not, and have never been, afraid of work,' she set the record straight, her tone marginally less heated.

'Then what is it you're afraid of?' he demanded. 'Is it the word "jungle" that alarms you?' he annoyingly probed.

Delfi tossed him a frustrated look. 'In all honesty I can't say that thoughts of spending a month in the jungle fill me with ecstasy,' she woodenly confessed. 'But it— isn't that...'

'So?' he insisted.

She gave him an exasperated glance, but with him being so persistent she got the feeling that he'd stay at her door all night if he had to, and that he wasn't leaving until she gave him an answer.

'If you must know,' she told him snappily, 'when I left England, I packed for an office environment.'

'I'm not with you,' he stated.

'A tailored outfit and high heels are going to look lovely where we're going!' she flared, and felt she could cheerfully have aimed a kick at his shins when, as light dawned, she caught a glimpse of the quickly squashed amusement that flickered in his expression.

He then glanced at his watch and to her irritation seemed, in moments, to have the answer to everything. 'There'll be no time later to get you kitted out,' he announced. 'We'll go now.'

'Now!' Delfi exclaimed, her eyes huge in her face.

'You can take two minutes to change out of your present garb first, if you prefer,' he drawled, his eyes scanning over her robe, with a trace of her nightdress where her robe opened just above her bosom.

'The shops are open at this time of night?' she queried, watchless but guessing that it must be about ten-thirty!

'The night market in Chiang Mai, so I've been told, is not to be missed,' he drawled, and suddenly Delfi started to latch on to the idea.

'I'll need ten minutes,' she told him hurriedly, and felt compelled to explain, 'I haven't got any make-up on.' For her sins, she drew his scrutiny to her clear, glowing skin.

'You, Miss Washington,' he remarked after several moments of studying her fine features, 'must know that you've a head start on most other women—without the aid of cosmetics.'

Delfi wasn't sure that she didn't reel back into her room. For a stunned second or two, she found it difficult to believe that he had, actually had, paid her a compliment! Was it possible that he'd actually hinted that he thought her—beautiful?

Realising that she'd got more urgent things to do than to look for compliments in anything McLaine said, Delfi hurried to get dressed. She suspected that he'd gone to the lounge area to wait, but she didn't doubt that he'd be back thumping on her door or—worse—change his mind about taking her, if she didn't get a move on.

Eight minutes after he had gone Delfi was flicking a comb through her hair, adding powder to her nose and, pausing only to pick up her bag, she was dashing from her room.

Boden McLaine was waiting for her when, having caught up with her breath in the time it took for the lift to descend, Delfi stepped from it. 'Sprint champion at school?' he murmured in recognition of how she couldn't have hung about.

Delfi fell into step with him and most oddly realised that he had reached her sense of humour. Suddenly, she felt like laughing.

A taxi dropped them off at the night market in Chiang Mai and Delfi was at once totally absorbed and fascinated. Traders selling all manner of goods occupied both sides of the street, with the market being so popular and crowded that it was only possible to shuffle along, walking at any ordinary pace out of the question.

'What kind of gear do you need?' Boden asked as they joined the shuffling throng.

'T-shirts, trousers, and some flat shoes should do it, I think,' Delfi replied, and was glad of his superior height when he at once spotted a T-shirt stall and guided her over to it.

The T-shirts were cheap, well made and quite a bargain. She selected half a dozen, but when she went to pay for them discovered that Boden had got there first.

'I'll pay,' she protested firmly, her wallet already in her hand.

'Put your money away,' he instructed smoothly, and when it looked as though she would argue the matter,

'Most employers pay for the company uniform,' he added, and suddenly he smiled—and Delfi put her money away.

He insisted on paying for the four pairs of trousers and the two pairs of canvas shoes, also, and added half a dozen pairs of socks which she hadn't thought of.

They were on the point of leaving the market when, held up by a crowd of people showing an interest in fake Gucci, Rolex and Cartier watches, Delfi was almost jostled off her feet by someone pushing to go in an opposite direction. She did not fall, however, because in an instant Boden was there, his arms firm about her as he plucked her a few steps away to a wall where there was a bit of space.

He still had his arms firmly around her when Delfi looked up to thank him. But—as she stared at him, no words would come. For suddenly her heart began beating like a trip hammer, and as he stared down into her wide eyes a tremendous tension seemed to transfer itself from him to her. Her lips parted, but no sound would come, and as his glance flicked from her eyes to her mouth, so, as though drawn to her, his head started to come down. Delfi felt certain that he was going to kiss her—and her heart began to beat even faster.

He did not kiss her—but even as his head came that fraction nearer he at the same moment turned his head away. In the very next moment, Delfi pushed at him—and spent the next couple of seconds battling with confusion and only returned to normality when, with his hand on her elbow guiding her, Boden grated, 'Where the hell are all the taxis?'

As if on cue a taxi, bearing occupants about to vacate, pulled up. A short while later—having exchanged not one word with Boden on the return journey—Delfi stepped from the taxi and went inside the hotel.

Boden joined her at the desk but was back to being his taciturn self when, unsmiling, he handed her some of the purchases he'd been carrying.

Silently, Delfi took the packages from him, then turned to accept her key from the receptionist. And, having thanked her, 'Goodnight,' she turned to bid her employer. He did not reply, but merely nodded. Clearly, he wasn't liking her very much.

Well, that went two ways, Delfi fumed, and stalked away from him furious. Surprisingly, though, as she sailed upward in the lift, she remembered the firm feel of Boden's arms around her, and remembered the way her heart had raced. Then she dwelt on how annoyed he had made her a few moments ago. Truly, she realised, he had the most exceptional power to disturb her—to make her moods swing rapidly first one way and then another. Now *why* the dickens was that?

CHAPTER FIVE

As soon as she was awake on Sunday morning, Delfi began to wonder what on earth had possessed her that last night she had imagined, for a moment, any of what she had about Boden McLaine. For goodness' sake, as if he'd been tense or had felt anything at all about her—apart, that was, from his usual irritation!

She went and had a bath, and was pulling on a pair of the previous evening's purchases when she discarded, too, any notion that he might have felt drawn to kiss her. Grief—as if he would! Heaven help us—as if she'd let him!

At that precise moment, she decided that she was in a hurry and had no time whatsoever in which to dwell on why her heart had raced the way it had when she'd been in his arms. She had, she determined, far more important things to do. The first of which was to start her month-long stint of being the perfect secretary.

Boden McLaine, she found, when she caught up with him, was not in his sunniest humour—Delfi was beginning to suspect she was never going to see the 'sunniest' side of him.

'Have you got your gear together?' he demanded when she joined him at his breakfast table.

'Every last T-shirt,' she replied evenly, not quite knowing herself how, when she had arrived with a full-to-capacity suitcase, she'd managed to add her newly acquired 'uniform' to it, and yet still, admittedly with some difficulty, been able to close it.

Very little in the way of conversation passed between them after that. Boden McLaine seemed very much preoccupied with his own thoughts, and Delfi, having made the effort to be pleasant, decided that she had done all that could be expected of her.

The flight to Chiang Rai took just over twenty minutes and they disembarked to be met by blistering heat. Delfi walked across the tarmac with her aloof employer and waited, as close-lipped as he by that time, for the arrival of their luggage. Then, having claimed their cases, they went outside the airport building again where he, ever a man who knew where he was going, aimed for a car park area and for a stationary Land Rover in particular.

'Sawadee, krub,' he bade good morning to the small, smiling Thai man who stood by the vehicle and seemed to be watching out for them.

After the Thai's beaming response, there followed a dialogue between the two men in Thai where Delfi heard Dr Phothiat's name mentioned, and where she realised that Dr Phothiat must have phoned ahead and arranged this transport for them.

Boden must have spent his spare time in mugging up some smattering of the Thai language, she realised, and had spent that time to good effect, because he and the Thai man appeared to be communicating very well.

Delfi watched as Boden signed for the Land Rover, then her luggage and his was being loaded into the rear, which was already mostly full with a miscellany of boxes and containers which she presumed Dr Phothiat had arranged for also.

Then Boden and the Thai man were shaking hands Western-style and, as the man waited to wave them off, Boden went round to the passenger door. 'If you'd like to get in,' he suggested to her pleasantly.

Somewhere Delfi had read that it was considered very bad form in Thailand to show anger. And so, when she felt more annoyed than angry that her taciturn employer should suddenly show himself to be the epitome of goodness and light, she dredged up her sweetest smile. 'Thank you,' she murmured quite beautifully—and, for good measure, she beamed at the Thai too, then climbed in.

Boden's slamming the door fast shut on her was more heavy-handed than light, she thought whimsically. When he appeared round at the driver's door and then climbed in beside her, he was back to being the monosyllabic brute he had been for most of the day.

For hours, then, or so it seemed to her, they motored in comparative silence. She owned that she was not looking forward to her month-long assignment but, since she had been paid—and paid well—she tried hard to look for pluses.

The greatest plus, of course, was that by staying in the north of Thailand with McLaine it was financing her self-imposed exile from England. She looked in front at the well-made, well-preserved tarmac road. Now that just had to be another plus. To hear Dr Phothiat talk last night, she'd have expected to be pushing the Land Rover out of some giant-sized pot-hole at any moment.

Her thoughts had drifted and she was admiring the greenery around and the wealth of acacia trees there seemed to be when Boden stated, 'We'll stop for lunch here.'

She glanced at her watch. It was one-thirty. 'Anything you say,' she murmured, having decided that, since Dr Phothiat had plainly been exaggerating, she would put up with the next month with every outward appearance of being pleased to be where she was.

The place where Boden had chosen for their lunch
stop was a surprise and delight in that it seemed to be
an area of well-preserved parkland. Flowers of red and
yellow abounded, and as she and Boden sat in the open
air and ate their meal a kind of peace started to wash
over her.

'How on earth did you find this super place?' she could
not resist asking him when the delightful sound of some
bird singing near by began to get to her.

'I can't claim the credit,' he replied evenly—she
awarded him half a point for replying at all and another
half that there was no sharp edge to his voice. 'Dr
Phothiat suggested it might be a decent place to stop—
before we turn off the main road.'

Delfi wasn't so sure that she was too thrilled about
that last bit. But, in the interest of continued harmony,
instead of enquiring further she opted to bury her head
in the sand. 'It's certainly beautiful here,' she
commented.

Less than an hour later she was discovering that she
had been premature in her opinion that Dr Phothiat had
been exaggerating. Soon after they had finished their
lunch, Boden had driven on again and had turned the
Land Rover off the main road and had begun to drive—
to her mind what could only be described as into the
hills.

In no time they were travelling over rutted red earth,
all sign of tarmac or man-made road gone, and with
thick foliage everywhere. They were high up, with hills
and valleys all about, and still climbing when Delfi realised what a misnomer the word 'pot-hole' was. They
weren't pot-holes, she mused; craters were what they
were!

'Hang on,' Boden ordered, and Delfi 'hung on' hard
to the rail in front as he steered to the left to miss one

enormous depression, and then gripped harder than ever and didn't know how she prevented herself from crying out when, choosing the wrong moment to look out of the side-window, she saw that there was a sheer drop! She swallowed hard and wanted to warn Boden of the danger, then knew that he was fully aware of it and had taken it into account. For he swung the vehicle to the right and, the danger past, he observed laconically, 'Not the screaming type, I see.'

Any tension that had been in her body immediately departed. Somehow it was as if he had a points system of his own and Delfi felt inordinately pleased, just as though he had awarded her top marks. 'Would I?' she shrugged, and was glad he'd no idea how close she'd come to calling out in fright.

Another five minutes of the tortuous, bone-shaking drive went by, then suddenly, out of nowhere, a youth on a motorbike passed them going in the opposite direction. Delfi wasn't sure why she should be so surprised to see the motorcyclist, because in the short time she'd been in Thailand she'd observed that the motorbike, for both men and women riders, was very popular.

However, having seen the youth, it gave her heart to suppose that they must be almost upon their destination. Her spirits were to dip though when only five or so minutes later Boden halted the Land Rover beside some tumbledown-looking shacks where some grubby and runny-nosed tots trailed after some bigger children who were busily engaged in a game of whip and top.

Oh, heavens, Delfi thought, as she glanced about the quite appalling place and tried to find something to recommend it. She found it in that the children looked as though they had plenty of energy for their game so must, she decided, be well and happy.

'Is this—er—where we're staying?' she asked, trying to keep all trace of anxiety out of her voice when he opened the driver's door and made to get out.

'We've some miles to go yet,' Boden answered, and went to talk to a couple of the older boys who then began indicating a track to the left.

From that Delfi gathered that Boden was confirming travel directions with the boys. Her heart, she owned, as Boden got back into the vehicle, was leaden. The laws of logic were insisting on telling her that the further they got away from civilisation it could only get worse—not better.

Her spirits were at a very low ebb therefore when, having got used to being jostled and bumped about as the Land Rover made its way over the tortuous road, the meandering dirt track suddenly deteriorated even more. Then the Land Rover hit such a bump that, short of being nailed down to her seat, Delfi stood no chance of keeping contact with it. Flung off balance, she went heavily against Boden, her long silver-blonde hair brushing against his face as she struggled to pull back from him. He was not pleased!

'Confound it, woman!' he bellowed, recovering from the surprise of having her very near catapulted on to his lap. 'Grip hold of the blasted rail, not me!' he thundered, and, while grimly keeping his right hand rock-steady on the wheel, he used his other hand to push her angrily away from him.

Feeling most unbearably hurt by his abrupt treatment of her, Delfi recovered her balance and moved as far away from him as she could. She looked fixedly out of the side-opening, the window long since having been opened as wide as it would go in order to have as much ventilation in the steamy heat as possible, and grappled with the unexpected sensation of hurt at Boden's treatment of her.

What she could not understand for quite some minutes was why she should have felt in any way hurt by him. After puzzling at it for a while, though, Delfi came to the conclusion that being so far away from home, and having no idea where she was going to lay her head that night—save that from what she'd seen so far she doubted that, wherever it was, it would earn any stars in any guidebook—she must be feeling most decidedly vulnerable.

Having satisfactorily dealt with that matter, she looked to the front again, and was just coming to the conclusion that if they travelled any further north they'd be across the Burmese border, when suddenly the area around started to look a deal less rugged.

As Boden began to slow the vehicle, she observed that there seemed to be a hint of civilised living in that, although still surrounded by hills, Boden was steering into a small encampment that looked particularly well cared for.

'Is—this it?' she dared to ask, and held her breath as she waited for his answer.

'This is it,' he confirmed, and Delfi didn't wait to hear any more. Quickly she made her escape from the Land Rover. With luck she wouldn't have to get back into it again until tomorrow.

'Mr McLaine!' A youth of sixteen or seventeen came hurrying over to them. 'I have waited all afternoon for you,' he beamed and, while he chatted to Boden, she looked about to observe that in the small clearing were three fairly widely spaced, straw-roofed, single-storeyed buildings. She saw the youth pointing to one of the dwellings that was built on the side of a hill and stood on stilts, having shorter stilts at the rear and, where the

hill sloped sharper, longer stilts at the front. She rather
gained the impression that that dwelling was the one that
had been reserved for them.

Boden confirmed it. 'Want a lift?' he queried drily,
plainly having decided to park the Land Rover nearer
to the accommodation.

'I'll walk over, thanks,' Delfi replied, repressing
severely any hint of a smile that her temporary employer
was quite well aware that there were certain parts of her
anatomy that felt quite numb.

While he and the youth, who'd said his name was Seri,
got into the Land Rover, Delfi moved to a footpath that
led up to the building. She wasn't quite sure how she
felt about sharing what she thought could be termed a
bungalow with Boden. Though, since the bungalow,
from outward appearances anyhow, seemed much, much
better than what she had imagined might be waiting for
her at the end of the journey, far be it from her to
complain.

The buildings were constructed of timber and of woven
cane, and each had a veranda, she noted, then halted in
her step and turned slowly about. There were mountains
all around, she saw, and lush green vegetation everywhere. She continued on her way, noting that all vegetation about the buildings had been severely cropped,
except for small attractive bushes which had been left
as an adornment around each stilt holding up the
properties. The whole scene, and atmosphere, Delfi felt,
was one of peace and beauty.

Trust Boden McLaine to find this idyllic spot tucked
away from the rest of the world. Her thoughts mean-
dered on to how he must surely have had to put the hours
in to make his business successful—what better place to
take a well-earned holiday than here!

Correction—his holiday would have been relaxing had his father not been called home. Unexpectedly, Delfi knew a moment of sympathy for Boden as she walked round the side of the cane-woven dwelling. If this was his annual holiday, and for him to be taking a month off she rather guessed that it was, then it wasn't going to be much of a break doing his father's work for him, was it?

Delfi rounded the corner of the building and saw that the Land Rover was parked outside. She then experienced a surprising rush of feeling that made her want to do everything she could for Boden to try and make it as much of a holiday as she could for him in the circumstances.

For crying out loud, she scorned a moment later, I must be going soft in the head! The ground had levelled out; she went up the path and, observing that the Thai youth had left his thonged sandals at the door, she kept to the custom of the country she was in, removed her shoes and then crossed over the entrance.

She found herself in what she took to be the sitting-room-cum-dining-room. There were a couple of rattan settees there anyhow, and also a dining table with several dining chairs. To the front of the room there was another door. The door stood open and light from the veranda spilled into the windowless room. To the right lay another door which was open and from which more light spilled. Outside that door stood her suitcase.

Delfi was just about to go towards that door when Seri came out, lifted up her case and disappeared inside with it. At the same time there was a sound to the left, and, turning, she saw Boden had come from a similarly open door on that side.

'You'll be as safe as houses here,' he commented as he took a couple of steps which brought him closer. 'But, just in case you feel the need,' he added, and with that he handed her a key.

'Wh...?' she began to ask, but just then Seri, barefoot, pattered from the door to the right.

'Your apartment is ready for you, Mrs Washington,' he announced happily, and, having had a little trouble with Washington, he scuttled off before she had the heart to tell him that she was Miss, not Mrs.

'Er—thank you,' she murmured, but wasn't sure whether she was thanking the absent Seri for his services, or Boden for the key.

'It'll be dark in about an hour,' Boden informed her. 'If you've any plans to take a shower it might be an idea to do so now.' And he seemed able to make out even in what natural light there was in the shadowy sitting-room that she wasn't sure what he meant. 'There's no electric light here,' he elucidated.

'Oh!' she exclaimed, and while wondering why she hadn't worked that out for herself she enquired, a shade fearfully it was true, 'But—there is hot water?'

'By courtesy of a cylinder of gas underneath the floorboards,' he answered, and left her to it.

Delfi went to investigate her 'apartment'. Boden, she gathered, had an apartment of his own on the other side of the sitting-room. She walked into a bedroom that had a giant-sized double bed. By the bed stood a bamboo table on which rested a candle in a candlestick and a book of matches. There was also a large bottle of mineral water, a bottle opener and a glass. So far, so good.

While absently observing that the bed-head was made of the same woven cane as the walls, Delfi realised that the partitioning was so thin that you could hear a pin drop in the next room. Though, since she otherwise had every degree of privacy, she was not concerned by the thinness of the walls. She was in the act of admiring a small, prettily patterned rug on the floor when she saw that in the places that the rug did not cover she could see daylight through the floorboards.

At least there was plenty of ventilation, she thought good-humouredly, and went over to the window aperture to see that while there was no glass there was a net roller-blind and also a shutter which presumably she would close at night.

Delfi completed her inspection by taking in that she had some wardrobe space, and that the bathroom to the two-roomed dwelling was little short of luxury when one considered how far away they were from civilisation.

The light was already starting to fade when she unearthed some fresh linen from her case, and went to shower. The water was beautifully warm and again she was of the opinion that the two-apartment dwelling would have been an ideal spot for Boden's holiday and his father's work.

She dried and dressed and lit a candle and then closed the shutters. Then the most terrible notion suddenly winged in out of nowhere. What if she was wrong and tonight, like last night, and the night before, they were merely in transit? Oh, no, she thought, and realised only then just how much she had taken to the place. Fate wouldn't be so unkind, would it?

From then, and for the next hour, Delfi fretted that she had assumed too much and that for every night of the next month she was going to find herself resting in some new abode.

She resolved finally that her first question when she saw Boden again would be to ask him. Consequently, as soon as she heard him leave his apartment, she left hers.

'Oh,' she said in surprise when, on going into the sitting-room, she saw that not only was the room well lit by hurricane lamps, but that the dining table had been laid for dinner. 'I didn't hear anyone come in,' she said, forgetting entirely in her surprise that she had been going to ask Boden a question.

'Seri came along with the lamps at about six,' he informed her easily. She'd been under the shower at that time, Delfi realised. 'He'll be along with dinner presently.'

'Does he have one of the apartments?' she enquired, seating herself on one of the settees.

'His family have the end one which is next to the kitchens,' Boden informed her, taking his ease in the other settee.

'Does he do the cooking too?'

Boden shook his head. 'His mother does the cooking, cleaning and laundry, while his father does a bit of logging or whatever else is going around. As well as attending to all the fetching and carrying, Seri keeps the grounds in order and makes sure the jungle doesn't encroach.'

'He speaks English very well,' Delfi stated.

'That's because his parents, who are hill people, wanted him educated. Having moved to a town in that endeavour, though, I believe they were quite pleased just the same when, the hills pulling apparently, he got this job and the family returned.'

Delfi decided that she quite liked Boden when he forgot to be a brute; it made her feel she could freely join in on any subject. Though it was the one they were discussing that still held her attention. 'You've learned a lot in a short time,' she remarked in pleasant fashion.

'You were having a shower when he came in to put a cloth on the table,' Boden commented, clearly having heard the running shower through the woven cane walls.

'Aside from wanting to practise his English, he's a talkative young man.'

'He sounds it,' Delfi agreed, and smiled suddenly because, having once—what seemed an age ago now—thought Boden had a kind streak in him, she felt that thought endorsed. Because, although she knew from experience what a curt brute he could be at times, he had allowed Seri to rattle on when had he felt like it he could have shut him up in no time flat.

She saw Boden's eyes flick down to her still-smiling mouth, but just when she remembered that she had a question to ask, Seri, leaving his flip-flop sandals at the door, came in bearing a huge tray.

'Dinner for you!' he announced with a sunny smile, first setting down the large square torch that dangled from a handle held by a couple of fingers beneath the tray. Delfi went forward to help him. 'I do, Mrs Washington,' he said quickly, in his haste making a worse mess over the name Washington.

Realising it must be a matter of pride with him, Delfi smothered her instincts to help, and watched instead as he deftly removed the covers from their meal, and looked to Boden to check that everything met with his approval.

'That looks fine, Seri,' Boden told him and as Seri beamed with pleasure, then went quickly away, Boden pulled out a chair at the table for Delfi. 'Since it seems we've been served a soup course and a main course at the same time, it might be an idea to get started,' he suggested.

Quickly Delfi took her seat, feeling then that she really liked Boden. Without question, he could quite easily have taken the smile from Seri's eager-to-please face by telling him that they would have preferred the main course to be held back and kept warm while they finished the soup, but he hadn't. Tomorrow he might, but tonight he hadn't, and Delfi suddenly realised that not only did she like Boden the better because of it, but that she respected him very much also.

But, in thinking of tomorrow, she remembered as she spooned soup to her mouth that she had a question she wanted to ask. There seemed no time like the present. 'Er—do we—um—move on again tomorrow?' she asked that which by then had become extremely important to her.

'You don't like it here?' he queried, setting down his spoon and looking at her sternly.

'Not that I'd dream of telling you otherwise,' she stated bravely, and solemnly, and then smiled that smile that again brought his glance to her mouth, 'but, in all honesty, I think it's absolutely beautiful here.'

'But you still want to move on tomorrow?' he insisted.

'Not at all!' she replied sharply, and, without knowing how he had so soon moved her to irritation, 'I've told you, I think this place beautiful. I love it here.'

For perhaps two seconds Boden stared at the pink flush of annoyed colour in her cheeks, then, his glance transferring to her sparking violet eyes, suddenly a slow smile started on his mouth. 'Perhaps, in the circumstances,' he said at last, 'that's just as well.' Then, his smile really making it, 'This is our base camp for the next month.'

'Truthfully?' she beamed.

'Would I lie?' he returned.

'Great.' Delfi smiled happily, and indeed felt so happy suddenly that she accepted that fact. After having been so down about matters in her private life, she wanted to savour that feeling of being happy again and had no intention of delving into the whys and wherefores of it. 'How did you manage to find such a superb spot?' she asked.

'I didn't,' he owned, and as the meal advanced he revealed that when his father had heard he was coming to Thailand for an exhibition he had put forward the holiday-research idea. His father had some time ago, however, decided that he had reached an age where he was no longer prepared to rough it—if it could possibly be avoided. To that end, he had contacted his old friend Dr Phothiat.

Delfi was aware as the meal finished that she had Boden's father, and of course Dr Phothiat, to thank for the fact that she was, and would be for the next month, in such delightful surroundings.

She had just got up from the table and was about to start stacking the used dishes when there was a tap on the door and Seri was there asking if it was convenient for him to clear away.

'Will you thank your mother for a lovely meal, Seri?' Delfi requested, and felt warmed to her heart at the happiness in his smile.

'I will, I will,' he stated emphatically, and went off grinning from ear to ear.

Most peculiarly, Delfi experienced the strangest sensation of shyness when he'd gone and she was again alone with Boden. How odd, she thought in confused astonishment, having spent the whole of the mealtime with him without feeling in the least bit shy.

'I think, since we're staying put for a month, I'll go and unpack,' she quietly told Boden.

'You'd better have one of these hurricane lamps,' he suggested, his tone even, quite obviously nobody nor nothing affecting him.

'I... Won't you need it?' she asked.

'There's enough light from this one for me to read,' he replied, and while Delfi comprehended that he would stay in the sitting-room with a book he reached up for

one of the lamps and carried it into the bedroom of her
'apartment'. Delfi followed him and watched as he placed
it on a hook that had been screwed into a wooden up-
right that also supported the woven cane wall. Then he
transferred his gaze to her, and stilled for a second or
so, then, 'Goodnight,' he said crisply, and went out,
closing the door after him.

The hurricane lamp was a great help, but with the cane
wall no more than a thin screen really, Delfi was very
much aware that the sounds as she walked back and forth
to the wardrobe must float into the next-door room and
could disturb his reading.

Having unpacked her 'uniform' clothes, she decided
to take the chance that they might return to base camp
before it was dark tomorrow. There'd be time then to
shake out and hang up anything 'eveningy' and not too
dressy, she thought. The rest, including her 'officey'
stuff, she could leave in her case and save her wardrobe
space.

Having come to that conclusion Delfi went and lit the
candle and took it with her to the bathroom, where she
washed and got into her nightdress. She then took the
lighted candle to the bedside table and, flicking her glance
back to the hurricane lamp, she thought for a second or
two about donning a robe and then going and asking
Boden to come and turn the lamp out. A moment later
she was telling herself not to be so pathetic, and a
moment after that, for all she'd never had experience of
a hurricane lamp before, she was going over to study it.

Two minutes later, the lamp was safely out. Giving
herself a mental 'well done' for achievement, Delfi, a
pleased look on her face, went to turn about, but got
only halfway when suddenly, as her glance caught a
shadowy corner of the room, so the hairs on the back
of her neck stood on end and, horror-struck, she froze.

For there, coiled up and waiting, was one very long—snake!

Boden had only that afternoon observed that she was not the screaming type, but Delfi afterwards realised, even though she was entirely unaware of it, that she must have made some cry of alarm. For, so swiftly that she was still rooted to the spot and staring huge-eyed and had not so much as moved a fraction, the door was suddenly crashed open and Boden was there.

The light in her room was not good, but, not wasting time with words, his eyes followed her hypnotised look, and as Boden at once saw the reason why she looked so petrified he—to make her blood run cold—took a step forward as though to examine the two-toned green reptile. Then, as if that weren't enough, he caused her such almighty fear that she almost went into heart failure by without more ado bending right down to it. Delfi had begun to shake uncontrollably before he straightened up. When he turned about, and she saw that he had the snake in his hands, she came the closest she had ever come in her life to fainting.

Boden did not waste time but strode promptly from her room. Vaguely, she heard the outer door open and close but, her fear not for herself but for him, she was never more glad than when in no time he was back again.

'Hey,' he murmured, when close to her he noticed the state she was in. 'It's all right,' he tried to tell her. But she was in shock and was barely hearing him, and he moved another step and put a calming arm around her shaking, nightdress-clad back. 'Saints preserve us,' he attempted to tease when the way she was shaking communicated itself to him, 'it was only a harmless long-nosed whip-snake,' he again tried to get through to her.

'W-was it?' Delfi asked, coming out of her shock at seeing the snake, but still shocked to the core at the intensity of feeling that had engulfed her when she had thought Boden's life in danger. 'Oh, Boden,' she couldn't prevent herself from crying on a shaky breath, and as he turned her in his arm so she should rest a moment against him she was awash with not only shock—but was in a quagmire of confusion too.

'It's all right now,' he repeated again from somewhere up above her head when, with both of his arms now about her, he tried to reassure her. 'He was harmless, I promise you—but he's outside now, and can't get back in.'

'I . . .' she attempted, but wasn't anywhere near herself yet—and, indeed, was beginning to feel that she would never be the same again.

'Come, now, Delfi,' Boden said kindly, 'lift your head and let me see your face.'

'I'm—all right n-now,' she tried to convince him, raising her head as requested, and attempting to smile, for all it was a very shaky effort.

'You feel it,' he remarked, her trembling still communicating itself to him. Then, as serious blue-green eyes searched into her wide and confused violet ones, he murmured, 'Oh, you poor little love,' and gently, in what she afterwards realised was a 'make it better' kiss, he touched his lips to hers.

On that instant of his mouth touching hers though Delfi's hands, which were somehow holding his waist, gripped tightly. He went to pull back, but she wanted, needed that contact with him, and she clung on, with both hands and lips.

She felt him hesitate, but it was only momentary, then she had that contact she needed, for he did not take his mouth away from hers, but stayed there, his mouth over hers warm, and gentle still.

'Oh, Boden,' she whispered shakily when he broke the kiss, and she moved her hands from the sides of his waist to put her arms all the way around him.

He pulled back and stared down into her deeply violet eyes. 'I have to go,' he told her, in a voice that reached her as being husky somehow.

'I know,' she said, but held on to him, and offered her lips for him to kiss again. 'G-goodnight,' she smiled.

His glance went from her eyes to her mouth. 'Oh-h . . .' he started on an agonised breath of sound, but as his arms about her tightened so his head came down again, and Delfi never heard what else he'd meant to add, for his mouth was occupied, as again he kissed her.

How many times he kissed her after that, Delfi had no idea. But soon the gentleness of his kisses was being replaced by a growing tide of passion, and as the shaking she experienced in her fear for him began to abate so she began to tremble, this time for a very different reason.

She was no longer afraid for him as he moved with her to her bed. Nor was she afraid of him. He had lighted a fire within her such as she had never known and she wanted him, with every fibre of her being.

'Boden,' she whispered his name as he lay down with her and, with his body half over hers, pressed her down into the mattress.

'I want you,' he murmured, his voice all throaty and as she'd never heard it before.

'Oh . . .' she sighed, and because she needed to feel his warm skin she stroked her hands around the back of his neck.

A groan escaped him. 'Delfi,' he whispered her name, and began to caress her body. She clutched on to him when with caring fingers his hands moulded her breasts, but she wanted more, much more.

She wanted to cry out again and again how much she needed him, wanted him, but there was then a mixture of shyness and need when, the thin covering of her nightdress getting in the way, he removed her covering, while his mouth trailed kisses over her face.

'You're beautiful, so beautiful,' he uttered, raising himself to stare down at the valleys and peaks of her naked body. 'Sheer poetry,' he breathed in an undertone as in the shadows and candlelight he held her in one arm, while his other hand caressed over her silken skin.

'I want to feel you too,' she told him shyly, and saw him smile.

He kissed her then, long and lingeringly, and Delfi lost all sense of time. She felt his fingers caressing the hardened tips of her breasts, and felt rapture when his lips took the place of his fingers and his mouth and tongue kissed and caressed the pink-tipped swollen mounds of her bosom.

'Boden!' She just had to call his name again, and delight was hers for, after a kiss that seemed to draw the very soul from her, she discovered that he had shed his shirt and trousers. 'Oh,' she sighed, enraptured when he pressed his hair-roughened chest against her pulsing bosom.

Boden had his hands in her long silver-blonde tresses and his pulsating body was over hers. Soon, she knew, he would take her, soon she would be his. A smile began in her heart.

But, when she had thought she was deaf to all other sound, suddenly into her highly aroused and passionate senses the sound of someone calling a hushed something began to penetrate. She tried to ignore it, but knew that Boden had heard it too, and, much though it seemed that he didn't want to hear it, the calling—though hushed—was persistent.

She felt Boden still, heard him mutter something but didn't know what it was. Then, 'Hell!' he grated, and she wanted to cry out 'No!' in protest, because with the calling coming nearer all the time she sensed that Boden was relinquishing the idea of making love to her.

She knew it for fact when, as that outside voice came again, Boden rolled from her and sat with his back to her on the edge of the bed. Don't go, she wanted to plead, but knew that it was too late.

'Will you be all right?' he asked, his voice gruff, and Delfi realised that it was all over.

Yet there was still that within her that wanted to tell him that no, she wouldn't be all right, and that he couldn't leave her, not like this. But pride, pride which she at that moment hated, came from somewhere. 'Grief, yes,' she heard her own voice airily, if huskily, state.

Boden didn't wait to hear any more. By radar he found his shirt and trousers and without so much as one backward glance he picked them up and swiftly left her.

Delfi had her eyes closed as the door shut to behind him. Anguish and heartache hit her full-square then. She wanted to cry out, but was aware that he would hear the smallest sound she made. Desperately, she turned over and buried her face in her pillow.

Oh, how had it happened? How had she ever come to fall—in love—with him?

CHAPTER SIX

DELFI was never more glad when dawn finally arrived. Moving silently, she left her bed at six o'clock, but felt exhausted from having just spent the longest night of her life.

Noiselessly she went and opened the shutters and let some daylight into her room. She still felt as confused as ever she had been, for with the coming of morning there was no change to that which fear for Boden had brought her: when she had seen him go forward to that snake she had been utterly terrified, *for him*, because she was in love with him.

The knowledge of her love for Boden McLaine had been with her throughout the long night. From a window she stared out at lush green vegetation, at tall trees with high mountains beyond, and knew that with the coming of day her feelings for him had changed not one iota. The strength of that feeling amazed her. It was so strong, so fierce, yet at the same time so tender—and it made ridiculous whatever it was that she thought she had felt for Hugh Renshaw. She wondered how she could ever have deluded herself that she was in love with her sister's fiancé. Then she heard the sound of Boden moving about—and promptly forgot all about Hugh Renshaw.

Knowing by then that Boden was not asleep and that she would not disturb him, she went and had a shower, and then returned to her room to don trousers and a T-shirt. Suddenly then she started to feel a little happier about everything. It was very much a fact that she was going to have to come to terms with the certainty that

Boden would never return her love. Oh, he might have desired her last night, but she'd be crass if she read anything more into it than that. But all at once it came to her that things could be very much worse. The day would come of course when she would have to say goodbye to him, but—that was a whole *four weeks* away!

Heavens, to think there had ever been a time when she had been reluctant to come north with him! Far from reluctant, she was now glad, glad, glad that she'd come! Glad that she was here, glad that today she would sit beside him in the Land Rover as they drove further into the mountains and the jungle. Glad to have this opportunity to spend more time alone with him. Glad, oh, so glad, of those four weeks.

Indeed, her only reluctance, as she took a deep breath and stretched out a hand to the handle on her door, stemmed more from memory of their lovemaking last night. Desire had not been one-sided.

Owning to feeling a trace awkward, Delfi grabbed at a moment of courage and stepped from her room into the sitting-room. But, when she could have sworn that Boden was in there—the room was empty. Her insides settled, and, uncertain what to do, she went out on to the veranda. Then, to make a nonsense of her insides again, she suddenly heard the soft footfall of someone entering the sitting-room.

She had left the veranda door open, and, turning quickly round, she felt scarlet colour flood her face. 'Good—morning,' she managed, and knew that, even in the relatively gloomy light of the sitting-room, Boden had observed her suddenly heightened colour—and was not pleased by it.

'Your breakfast will be here shortly,' he told her curtly, by way of answering her greeting.

'My... What about your breakfast?' she asked, her glad spirits starting to get damp at the edges.

'I've eaten,' he answered crisply, his reply all Delfi needed to know that he wasn't feeling very sociable this morning—she, or probably her eagerness to be made love to the previous evening, the cause.

'I—see,' she said slowly, and began to feel just a tiny bit cross. So all right, she had been eager, but he hadn't been so very backward, had he? She took a steadying breath, and strove hard to be businesslike when she went on to add, 'I'll not need much in the way of breakfast, so I won't keep you long if you want to make an early start.' His reply left her gaping.

'You're not coming,' he announced curtly.

'I'm not...' She couldn't believe it. 'But—why?' she just had to ask.

'You'll be quite safe here,' he replied.

Which to her mind was no sort of answer. 'Why can't I come with you?' she insisted, and had to withstand his look of pure exasperation.

'Because you can't,' he rapped toughly.

'But——' she began—she wasn't having that for a reply either.

'The thought of the jungle terrifies you, for one thing,' he flung back in her face that which she had been weak enough to reveal she had not been too ecstatic about.

'I'm supposed to be your secretary,' Delfi reminded him stonily, valiantly hiding her hurt that by the sound of it Boden had gone off her in a big way.

'So I'll give you some dictation when I get back!' he snarled, and, clearly having had enough of arguing that which in his view there was no arguing about, he turned and went striding towards the outer door.

Delfi had moved back into the sitting-room by the time he came back and she realised that he had only gone outside to the Land Rover to collect something. She halted in her tracks, and her eyes followed him as she watched as he strode over to the dining table and set down the antiquated typewriter he was carrying.

'What's that?' she roused herself to question incredulously, if a shade belligerently.

'I thought you said you could type!' he challenged.

'I can!' she flared, not caring very much that he was back to doubting her abilities. 'But that machine must have come out of the *Ark*! I'm used to an electronic——'

'I'd have thought, Miss Washington,' he snarled woundingly, 'that you might—with *your* intelligence—have worked out by now that even the latest in the electronic or thermotronic typewriting equipment would be less than useless to you in the absence of an electricity supply.' Delfi hadn't surfaced from his stinging sarcasm, when, 'Instead of sitting around bellyaching about your lot, spend the day resurrecting your skills on a manual typewriter,' he grated, 'i.e.,' he rapped bluntly, refusing to let her get an angry word in edgewise, 'get some practice in!'

With that, pausing only to drop off a box of stationery, he got into the Land Rover and roared off. Swine, Delfi was left alone to becall him, to hate him, and to gather from his 'get some practice in' that he intended to keep her nose well and firmly to the grindstone.

She was still mentally damning him when five minutes after the angry sound of the vehicle had faded Seri appeared with her breakfast. *'Sawadee, krub,'* she rose over her emotions to find a smiling greeting for the youth. But was at once a little perplexed when he broke up in giggles. 'Didn't I say it right?' she questioned, knowing that her accent was far from perfect, but certain that

that was the greeting which she'd heard Boden use at the airport yesterday.

'Men say *sawadee, krub*,' Seri explained, 'but ladies must say *sawadee, kha*,' and beaming, '*Sawadee, krub*, Mrs Washington,' he grinned.

'*Sawadee, kha*, Seri,' Delfi caught on fast, though since he again had a bit of difficulty with her surname she suggested that he called her Delfi.

'Thank you, thank you, Mrs Delfi,' he immediately took up to make her smile, and unloaded his tray of orange juice, bacon and eggs, toast and coffee on to that part of the dining-room table that was clear. At the same time he chatted merrily away, telling her that he would call later for any laundry she had, and, his smile for once gone, he expressed the hope that he had not disturbed her last evening when his mother had sent him looking for his pet.

'You have a dog? A cat?' Delfi queried, and saw she had brought about a fit of the giggles again.

'Preecha is not a dog or a cat,' he informed her as he got over his giggles.

'Preecha?' she enquired, the name striking a chord as that being the word she had heard being called last night when she'd been in Boden's arms—'disturbed' hardly the word to describe the uproar of her—until then— dormant emotions.

'Preecha is my snake,' Seri revealed proudly. 'He is harmless,' he went on quickly, in case she should be alarmed. 'But, when he wasn't where he should be, my mother tells me I must find him straight away. She was afraid,' he confided, 'that Preecha might have come in here and hidden under the bed when she was here yesterday preparing for you.'

'You—er—found him?' Delfi asked as evenly as she could.

'Oh, yes.' Seri beamed happily. 'He was not—um—far away.'

Delfi went to the table after he'd gone, heartily wishing that she'd known in advance that Preecha was harmless. She drank some orange juice, but had no appetite at all for bacon and eggs. Not wishing to offend Seri, or his mother, though, she ate what she could. Any gladness she had felt earlier to be there with Boden had disappeared, and she saw the day stretching out long and endlessly as the night had done.

Delfi filled that day by emptying her suitcase of everything, repacking half of it, and then, while keeping close to the small clearing, by going exploring. In this way she came across Seri's mother, a youngish woman still who, like her son, was full of smiles. Seri's mother spoke no English, and Delfi spoke no Thai, but that seemed no barrier to friendship. Delfi went on her way having communicated her name to the youngish matron, and, if she'd got it right, having been invited to call Seri's mother by her first name which she thought was Aurapin.

The first thing Delfi saw when she entered the communal sitting-room of the two-apartment dwelling was the typewriter. With the aggressive way Boden had spoken to her that morning still sawing away at her, she threw the typewriter a look of intense dislike, then opening all doors so as to have maximum light she went over to it and 'resurrected' her typewriting skills.

She was back to being in love with Boden again when, as the light began to fail, she first heard then saw the Land Rover return.

'Did you have a good day?' she enquired pleasantly when he walked into the sitting-room.

'Was that supposed to be a joke?' he rounded on her before she could take another breath.

Too late she observed that he looked hot and tired and guessed he'd had to get out of the Land Rover and do some kind of running repair or other. But she'd been snarled at by him at the start of the day and, to her way of thinking, once a day was quite sufficient.

'Serves you right!' she snapped, and as he slammed into his apartment so she, not knowing why she was battling against sudden tears when she hated him so much, slammed into hers.

A few minutes later Delfi had regained her self-control, but had no intention of returning to the sitting-room to await his deigning to speak to her. She heard him taking a shower and, having come across a waterfall that day which by some means or other fed the domestic water tanks, she decided that, since there was no water shortage, she'd take a shower—her third that day—too. As she passed by a window though Delfi, as much as she hated Boden, couldn't help but be pleased to see that Seri was heading in the direction of their abode with a tray. Boden, she guessed, could do with something refreshing to drink.

When at around seven that evening she heard Seri again come in, she pinned an aloof 'touch-me-not' look to her expression and left her apartment. It was a waste of effort. Boden was instructing Seri on some provisions he wanted to take with him the next morning, and did not so much as glance her way. Ignoring him in turn, and noting that the typewriter had been transferred to a temporary home on the floor, Delfi went and sat down at the table.

Dinner was a silent affair. Since all Boden had done when he had spoken to her since last night was to be snarling and sarcastic, that was fine by her. That he was today regretting like hell having kissed her was obvious, painfully obvious. But he couldn't be regretting it any more than she.

'If you're ready,' he opened the moment she had drunk the last of her coffee, 'we can get down to some work.'

'I'll get some paper and a pen,' she replied smartly.

She had not been wrong, she discovered, in thinking that he intended to keep her nose to the grindstone. Her shorthand speed was good. It needed to be, for it seemed he expected only the best from her.

'That's all,' he coolly declared when she was beginning to think that she was never going to get to her bed that night. 'Don't worry if you get stuck with any of the alien spelling— I'll check it back tomorrow.'

And, on that kind word given, but taken back in that it seemed he wouldn't countenance the work not being done by the time he arrived back tomorrow, Delfi went to bed.

A week later, Delfi had typed her way through sheets and sheets of paper on the clackety-clack manual typewriter. By then she had worked up quite a speed, but she still didn't look on it as her favourite machine.

She guessed that Boden found her work acceptable— she was certain that she would have heard about it should he have some fault to find. He never gave praise but, since he'd paid her well, she reckoned that she had no cause for complaint.

That was, she wouldn't have minded had he unbent a little, and, well, shown her a little—friendliness. Not that she wanted him to kiss her again—heaven forbid. She'd learned the hard way that she was much too vulnerable in that area. Never had she thought that any man should have her as mindless as Boden had, when all he'd done at the start was to place a gentle kiss on her mouth.

Abruptly Delfi pushed what were now painful memories away from her. She leaned back in her chair and rested for a few moments from the physical exertion of typing, at speed, on the antiquated typewriter.

She sighed as she thought sadly of her love for Boden, and how, the way things were going, he would, at the end of her stint of work for him, probably walk away without so much as another glance.

A few seconds later she tried to oust him from her mind by concentrating on other thoughts. She had no idea how long it took the mail to reach England but any day now her family should receive the long and cheerful letter she had written and which Seri, on a shopping expedition on his motorbike, had taken to post for her.

Delfi had a few moments' respite from such constant thinking of Boden when, wonder and a trace of amusement still there, she recalled how with his motorbike piled high—appearing to be carrying everything but the kitchen sink—Seri had returned quite some hours later.

The vision of Seri and his bike abruptly evaporated when she recalled how, when he'd brought dinner over that night, he'd smilingly informed her that her letter was safely in the post.

'Who are you writing to?' Boden, to her astonishment, had had the nerve to ask.

Indeed, so astonished was she that she'd answered him before she'd given herself time to think about it. 'My family,' she had replied, then added tartly, 'They'll be pleased to know I've landed such a good job.'

'You can quit any time you like,' he'd snarled.

For a moment her breath had gone at his uncaring manner. Then, 'As you once reminded me,' she'd bounced angrily back, 'I'm broke!' and, having left him in no doubt that he wouldn't see her heels for dust if the job were voluntary and unpaid, 'I'm also starving,' she had lied and went and took her place at the table.

And so she had worked on. Saturday or Sunday, it made no difference to him. Off he went in the early hours, to return around dusk. Delfi was not sure if it was the facts of the work he did or his phraseology in putting it all together, but bit by bit she began to find it getting more and more interesting. So much so that, only yesterday, she had experienced an almost overwhelming desire to go with him and to see for herself the Mussur tribe with their black tribal dress trimmed with white and red and still worn today. But, however much she wanted to go and see for herself, she would not ask—she'd cut her tongue out sooner.

The thought that Boden would have another load of work for her when he returned was sufficient to bring Delfi back to earth and, her brief respite over, she again put her physical energies to work.

In fact, he seemed to have more work for her than ever when he started dictating that night. When the hour passed when he usually finished and he was still giving her dictation, and as Delfi's right hand started to seize up, she just had to halt to shake the cramp out of it.

She then very nearly dropped with shock when, observing what she was doing, he came close to apologising! 'I'm no expert in these matters, so I'm probably doubling up on facts which my father already has. But, since I can't get hold of him to ask, I'm afraid that this is the way it has to be.'

'Think nothing of it,' Delfi replied cheerfully, and, while aware that every neatly typed page she completed would ultimately be handed over to his father, she lived for the next few days on the crumbs gleaned that Boden had actually unbent sufficiently to as near as damn it apologise.

Delfi left her room on Saturday morning knowing Boden was in the next-door room and eager for a glimpse of him before he went off for the day. She entered the sitting-room just as Seri arrived with her breakfast.

'Good morning,' she said generally, while at the same time she was overwhelmingly aware that Boden had his eyes on her and seemed to be taking in the way she had—as was now usual—tied her hair back for coolness. She had given up wondering about the new emotions she was prey to since she had fallen in love with him. But, as she experienced a sudden—and to her mind, most ridiculous—moment of shyness, she felt the need to say something, anything, to get her over it. She glanced across to where Seri was transferring dishes from his tray on to the table—and said the first thing that came into her head. 'Is it today that you go into town shopping, Seri?' she asked him.

'You wish to come with me on my motorbike, Mrs Delfi?' he asked, brimful of pride about his machine as he beamed at her.

Delfi did not want to go with him on the back of his motorbike, but as she opened her mouth ready to tactfully thank him for his generous offer, and refuse, to her astonishment she heard Boden, *untactfully*, refuse for her!

'No, Miss Washington doesn't want to come with you,' he told him shortly, and while Seri, looking quite crestfallen, hurried from the room, so any trace of tranquillity Delfi had found over the last few days abruptly vanished.

'Why did you tell him that?' she hotly challenged.

'Did you want to go with him?' he rapped.

'That's not the point!' she flew, twenty-two and well able to make her own decisions without any help from him.

'Huh!' he scoffed, and ice there in his eyes suddenly, 'The point is,' he took up, his chin jutting aggressively, 'that you're not going anywhere on the back of any motorbike!'

Delfi saw red. He might be able to boss her about when her work was concerned, but that was all. 'Why not?' she demanded furiously.

'Apart from the fact that since he has no crash helmet for himself it's unlikely that he'll have one for you, because— *I* say so!' And as she stared at him not believing he'd just said what he had, 'Got it?' he thundered.

'You...' Delfi began in fury, but she was talking to the air. He had slammed aggressively out. 'Bossy, cantankerous swine,' she mutinied, then heard the angry roar of the Land Rover starting up. Damn his work, she fumed, and determined to take the day off.

She felt too angry to eat, but because Seri's feelings might already have been hurt once that day she did her best to get some of her breakfast down. To her relief, however, Seri was back to being his smiling self when he returned to collect her breakfast dishes.

'I should not have said you could come with me on my motorbike today,' he happily brought the subject up. And while Delfi was still searching for some way to excuse Boden's short tone with him—hate him though she might at that moment, love and loyalty went hand in hand—Seri went on to cheerfully explain, 'My mother says that I have work here to do today, and that shopping can wait.'

Delfi smiled when he had gone. By the sound of it, Seri had not been at all upset at the way Boden had spoken to him. Her smile quickly faded, though, and she was again annoyed with Boden that, even if she had decided to defy his 'because— *I* say so' and take a ride

on the back of Seri's motorbike, she couldn't—because
Seri wasn't going anywhere.

Finding that last thought extremely galling, Delfi
slammed into her typewriter and had achieved quite a
bit of work before she remembered that she had decided
to take the day off.

She supposed, though, that she must still be feeling a
shade rebellious when, after lunch, she thought that
having worked the previous Saturday and Sunday she
was justified in not returning to work. She would catch
up tomorrow.

The day was hot. She had a shower and washed her
hair and, dressed in fresh trousers and T-shirt, she opted
to take a walk and to let her hair dry in the sun.

Her walk took her further than she had walked before,
but when she had no intention of wandering further and
risking the likelihood of getting lost in the jungle she
suddenly heard the sound of Seri talking to someone.
Since that someone wasn't contributing anything to the
conversation, she guessed that he was talking to his pet
snake, Preecha.

Having regained her nerve where that particular reptile
was concerned, Delfi took a few steps away from the
path and into the dense undergrowth. Then her eyes
widened with surprise. It wasn't the long-nosed whip-
snake Seri was talking to, but a huge elephant!

'Mrs Delfi!' Seri caught sight of her and exclaimed,
and, all smiles, 'You want to ride on the elephant?'

'I wouldn't dare,' she replied, which seemed to amuse
Seri greatly, for he laughed his giggly laugh.

'But yes, you must! It will make me feel the better
that you could not ride my motorbike today.'

Delfi wished he had not reminded her of her non-
motorbike ride. She was tempted. 'Perhaps the elephant
wants a rest?' she suggested.

'He'd rather have some bamboo leaves and I know where there are some.'

A good few minutes later, Delfi, having gone with Seri to where there were a couple of close-together tree stumps, one higher than the other, climbed up on to the elephant's neck. She had her feet gently tucked in behind his ears, and, assured by Seri that the elephant wouldn't even notice her weight, she spent the first five minutes of travel in being certain that she had made an exceedingly foolish mistake. The ground looked a mile away and, with the elephant bending his head and stretching out his trunk to take a mouthful of any tasty titbit they happened to pass, she could only be very, very glad that Seri was walking beside her holding what amounted to a leading-rein.

In the following ten minutes, however, she had got used to the slow side-to-side swaying of the elephant, and started to enjoy it. Her alarm was much less at any rate when he dipped his head mid-forage. She began to look about her. Everywhere was green. Mountains still towered above the tree-tops, and although Seri had explained that the elephant was one who normally helped his father in the logging area, though was apparently not needed just then, she could see no sign of any logging area.

With the elephant's pace slow—bamboo leaves being its passion—it was nearly two hours later that Delfi spotted the clearing through the jungle where the small encampment was. She had enjoyed her ride, but she was nevertheless not unhappy that it was about to end.

Her thoughts immediately went to Boden and how he'd probably be in such a foul mood that she hadn't finished her work that she'd never get the chance to ask him, since motorbike rides were off secretarial limits, how he felt about elephant rides. Then, as they broke through from jungle into the clearing, she suddenly saw him. He was back early!

Seri brought the elephant to a standstill, but, even as her heart started to race, oh, crumbs, Delfi thought, for Boden, after pausing in his stride, had started to walk over to them. She guessed that any minute now she was going to get the sharp edge of his tongue.

Trying to look more composed than she felt, but well aware of her hair loose about her, Delfi sat exactly where she was as Boden came and halted at the side of her.

Silently she looked at him but could find nothing to say. Even Seri seemed stuck for words when for ageless moments, or so it seemed, Boden just stood and looked back at her. Then, when she had been fully expecting to hear something loaded with acid, a warm look suddenly came to his blue-green eyes. And, as she watched in wonder, all at once the corners of his mouth started to pick up and Boden, magnificently and superbly— grinned!

Delfi couldn't believe it, and her heart was positively racing when, his tone as warm as his look, he drawled, 'Well, well. Whatever happened to the Miss Adelfia Washington I knew who was terrified of the jungle?'

'Terrified' was perhaps overstating it a bit, but at the warmth emanating from him her heart began turning cartwheels. Her lips parted, and she could do absolutely nothing about the matching grin that just would not be held down.

Which left her able to make the only reply possible in the circumstances. 'Shut up,' she laughingly told him.

To her joy, he remained in good humour. 'Come down here and say that,' he challenged, and when Delfi laughingly looked about for something that might resemble a stepladder he suddenly held up his arms.

Her heart was racing to beat all records when, first changing her astride position to one of side-saddle, she took a steadying breath, then put her trust in Boden.

He did not let her down. In the following instant of Delfi propelling herself forward, he caught her. Strong arms came firmly about her and held her while she got her balance—and Delfi was in heaven. Her arms went around him, and, as he held her, so she held him. She was in his arms, where she wanted to be, and that he did not seem in any hurry to let her go was bliss, pure bliss. Oh, Boden, I love you, I love you so, she thought, and felt totally secure in his firm hold.

Belatedly then, though, she came to her senses and was at once in an inner panic lest she had given away even the smallest hint of how much she cared for him. She moved her hands to his waist, and pushed back from him. Immediately, and to show just how much the clinging together had been one-sided, Boden not only straight away dropped his arms from her, but took a step away.

Delfi, striving hard for normality, suddenly spotted Seri silently watching them. 'Thank you very much, Seri,' she smiled. 'That was lovely.'

'*Mai pen rai,* Mrs Delfi,' he beamed, which she had by then learned meant 'you're welcome', and began to lead the elephant away.

'So—you've taken to elephant riding while my back's turned?' Boden remarked when by unspoken mutual consent they began to walk up a gradient to their apartments.

At the suggestion of teasing in his voice, life was suddenly wonderful again. 'That was my first ride,' she answered honestly. And, because Boden had been working and she hadn't, she felt obliged to own, 'I didn't feel much like working this afternoon.'

'You're not ill?' he looked at her sharply to rapidly enquire.

'No, not at all,' she instantly replied. 'I just—er—thought I'd like a change. I'll catch up tomorrow,' she promised as at the outer door of their abode they stopped to remove their shoes.

Delfi's heart was singing when she showered in her bathroom. Were the walls not so terribly thin, she might well have burst into song. But she restrained herself, and wondered again about this magical thing called love that just to see a smile on Boden's face, to be teased by him, should make her world suddenly sun-filled.

She was in a happy frame of mind when later she left her room to join him for dinner. The hurricane lamps illuminated the sitting-room-cum-dining-room as usual, so she was careful to avoid breaking out into smiles at the least opportunity. Though with Boden still in a superb humour—he was being very pleasant to her anyway—it was not always easy to hold down the wayward upward curve of her mouth.

She thought, however, that she had managed fairly creditably as they ate their way through *gai ob nam kati*, a speciality of Seri's mother and which was roast chicken in peanut and coconut sauce. They had seemed to have discussed anything and everything by the time they were drinking coffee. And Boden had that teasing expression on his face again when he asked, 'I hardly dare mention it, but does your having the afternoon off include this evening?'

Oh, Boden, is it any wonder that I love you? she thought, and swiftly hid her expression by leaving the table and collecting paper and pen. 'Ready when you are,' she said lightly, and loved him the more when he smiled.

From then on it was all work, though he did not give her so much dictation that night. That could have been because he knew that she still had some typing left over from that day, but Delfi was minded to think that it was because, having returned early that day himself, he had not done so much research as usual.

In any event, she had just taken down the last paragraph when she became aware that he seemed to have something on his mind. Her glance stayed on him and, though she hadn't meant to smile encouragingly, she guessed that she had, because suddenly he was stretching back casually in his chair and, with his long legs out in front of him, he was remarking conversationally, 'You never *did* tell me why it was that you left England in such a rush.'

From memory he'd had a good stab at guessing before—not that she could recall having told him that she'd left in so much of a rush. Suddenly, though, she was starting to feel wary. From what she could remember of the last time they'd had a discussion of this sort, they had both ended up angry. She didn't want that. She wanted Boden to stay the pleasant and good-humoured person he'd been all evening.

'There's—not a lot to tell,' she eventually replied, and smiled, because it really was rather ridiculous to suppose that she and Boden were unable to discuss this particular subject without heat.

'But you did have good reasons for wanting to leave?' he persisted.

She wished that he would drop the matter and wanted to beg him, Please don't ask. For, in truth, she was not feeling very proud of herself over Hugh Renshaw, and did not want Boden to see her in a bad light.

'You left because of some man, of course.' Boden seemed determined to get it all out of her, the sharp edge appearing in his voice because she was taking so long to answer, Delfi realised.

'You know that much,' she answered, and hated herself as much as she was hating his questioning because a sharp edge was coming into her tones too.

'Who was he?' he demanded to know.

'No one you know!' Delfi flew.

'You ran away because he didn't return your feelings?' He seemed hell-bent on needling her—and succeeded.

Damn him, he was making it sound as though he couldn't believe that any man could love her. 'And that's just where you're wrong!' she snapped.

'He loved you?' he insisted on knowing, his face darkening with aggression.

'So he said!' Delfi replied tartly, uncaring by then that he was looking aggressive because he didn't like the snappy way she was behaving.

'And you,' he snarled, 'you loved him?'

'Yes!' Delfi erupted, fed up with his needling. 'Yes, yes, yes!'

She caught the dangerous glint in Boden's eyes as he abruptly got up out of his chair, and turned his back on her. But, just when she started to draw a relieved breath that, by the look of it, for all he seemed furious that she was not some meek and mild secretary, he had done with questioning, he turned back.

'So why run?' he barked. 'What was so wrong about your love...?' He broke off, then charged, 'His wife wouldn't give him a divorce, would she?'

'For your information,' Delfi flared angrily, 'he wasn't married.'

'What, then?' He refused to let go, a man clearly who, having decided he wanted the bare bones, would not let up until he'd got it all, as he pushed her to be too furious then to care.

'If you must know,' she hissed, outraged, 'he is engaged to my sister.'

As soon as the words were out, Delfi wanted them back, for Boden stilled, looked at her long and hard, and then, without another word, he turned and went out into the night.

Delfi stared after him for several stunned and unhappy minutes after he'd gone. She had not wanted him to see her in a bad light, but it was obvious that he was so disgusted with her that he couldn't even bear to stay in the same building with her, let alone the same room!

Her spirits were at rock-bottom when Delfi crossed to her apartment. She found Boden's disgust dreadful to live with, and could find little compensation from the thought that, if he believed she was in love with someone else, then he was never in a month of Sundays going to so much as suspect that she was in love with him.

Without putting a match to a candle to light her room, Delfi undressed and got into bed. So much for her sun-filled world!

CHAPTER SEVEN

BODEN'S disgust with Delfi was a painful force the next day. Not that she saw such a great deal of him. He breakfasted early, and, when her need to see him overcame her reluctance, she stepped from her room just as he was leaving—though he barely cared to greet her. 'Good morning,' she addressed him coolly, seeing from his indifferent glance that she couldn't hope for a return of any of last night's earlier pleasantness.

The fact that he'd inclined his head by way of acknowledgement before going out to the Land Rover was something, she supposed gloomily. She worked hard that day, but proudly waited for Boden to be the first to speak when in the late afternoon he arrived back. Much good did it do her. She went to bed that night with the sum total of any conversation being, for the most part, the dictation he had given her.

The next five days followed the same pattern, but it was on Friday night that Delfi, sleepless in her bed, began to rebel. Love the swine she might, but she couldn't help it if she'd fooled herself into believing that what she'd felt for Hugh Renshaw was real love. Perhaps she had been wrong to imagine herself in love with her sister's fiancé, but she hadn't hung around to ruin her sister's happiness—so what was Boden McLaine doing giving her the cool, disdainful treatment?

Delfi spent a wretched sleepless night but was up early the next morning. That morning, however, she was still feeling mutinous against Boden, and though it was a hard fight not to leave her room to catch a glimpse of him before he left for the day she managed to win that particular battle.

She was, as she might have known she would be, full of instant regrets the moment that she heard the Land Rover drive away. Now she wouldn't see him until late afternoon. Delfi sighed and got on with her day.

Her surmise that she would see Boden again at his usual time of returning proved false, however. It was dark, and Seri had brought her dinner, and there was no sign of him.

'I will bring dinner for Mr McLaine later,' Seri told her with his ever-present smile.

'Thank you, Seri,' Delfi murmured, and held down the hundred and one questions she wanted to ask him—all centred around the theme, did he think that Mr McLaine was all right?

She had eaten little of her dinner, and Seri had been in and cleared away, and there was still no sign of Boden when Delfi went out on the veranda to watch for a sign of the Land Rover.

Her anxiety peaked when visions of Boden lying injured somewhere refused to budge. But, just when she'd decided that she didn't care if Boden did think her a panicking idiot, she was going to ask Seri to take her on the back of his motorbike to look for him, so, to her heartfelt relief, she saw the lights of the Land Rover flickering away in the trees. She hastened inside.

But so tremendous was her relief that she was still in the throes of wanting to fling her arms around Boden and check for herself that he had come to no harm when she heard the Land Rover pull up outside.

Delfi decided she'd better make herself scarce and swiftly left the sitting-room. She heard him come in, heard him moving about. Then she heard Seri bring Boden his dinner, and thought that if she did go out into the sitting-room he would soon start giving her some shorthand. She stayed put for two reasons. The one, because she thought he'd done enough work for one day; the other because, still feeling quite soft about him inside, she didn't think she could take a continuation of his hostile attitude—not tonight she couldn't.

She went and showered and got into bed, but sleep was, as last night, far away. She later checked her watch in the light of the candle—it had gone midnight, she saw.

She was of the opinion that Boden had been asleep for ages when unexpectedly a stray sneeze caught her out. Then, floating through the thin partitioning, wonderfully, marvellously, and like music to her ears, 'Bless you!' she heard Boden call.

Oh, my love, my love, she silently sighed, you're awake too. Strangely then, just as if she had needed his 'Bless you!', she went straight to sleep.

She awakened from the best night's sleep she'd had in months with Boden's 'Bless you!' still in her ears. Her candle had burnt itself out, but, suddenly afraid that Boden might have left, she went and raised the shutters and checked her watch. With relief, she saw that although it was daylight it was still early.

Quickly she got washed and dressed and as quickly brushed her hair. Then, telling herself that, since Boden had not given her any dictation last night he might want to do so this morning, she left her room.

He was just finishing off his breakfast, she saw, but not wanting to risk a rebuff if he was still hostile—the 'Bless you!' being nothing but an automatic response— she greeted him evenly, 'Good morning.'

'Good morning, Delfi,' he responded easily, to her joy. And, with a flicked glance to her silver-blonde hair loose about her shoulders, he—to her surprise and great delight—casually suggested, 'Since you're up so early, and since you appear to have lost the aversion you once had for the jungle, perhaps you'd like to come with me today and see at first hand something of the work you've been doing.'

Swiftly realising that he'd think she'd gone stark staring mad if she suddenly attempted a couple of double somersaults at his most marvellous invitation, 'That should be quite interesting,' she restrained herself to accept politely, heartily glad that he must have come to the conclusion he had on seeing her coming out of the jungle on an elephant. She delayed breaking out into the widest of smiles until later in the privacy of her room when she went to pick up her bag.

She had, during her time of working for Boden, typed reams on the Lisaw tribe, the Yao and the Kaw. She felt that she knew by heart where each tribe originated from, the Lahu or Mussur from southwest China, the Kariang or Karen from the west, across the Salween river in Burma, other tribes from Burma's Shan states in the north, or from over the Mekong river in Laos. But that day when, after driving over roads which she would have thought undrivable over, they eventually came to a hill-tribe village, Delfi was little short of entranced.

'We'll have to find the headman,' Boden informed her, but had little trouble in locating him since the arrival of the Land Rover brought out all and sundry.

In no time they were being made most welcome, and Delfi was going with Boden along with a procession of curious villagers to the headman's house. After that there was so much to take in and absorb. There were many dwellings all built of bamboo with straw roofs, with all of the dwelling being built on stilts.

She sat patiently while Boden conversed in Thai and hand-signs with the headman. She could understand not a word of what was being said, but kept her eyes open knowing that when Boden dictated back to her that evening it would all come alive again.

When a woman of about sixty appeared wearing a tall traditional headdress of beaten silver, fur and beads and a heavily embroidered tunic dress and signed that she should go with her, Delfi looked to Boden for guidance.

'Go with her,' he instructed her pleasantly, and added, 'Male visitors aren't allowed in the women's section.'

Happy just to have Boden being so pleasant with her, Delfi followed the woman out of the bamboo hut. She was thereafter little short of amazed that, when outside the village there was so much greenery of forest and jungle, inside the village there was so little.

From what she could tell most of the greenery had long since gone, and the village compound now stood on a hard dirt floor. She walked up what she guessed was the main street, skirting chickens who pecked at the red earth where as far as she could see there was nothing to peck at, and black pot-bellied pigs and piglets who rooted at the hard ground and who somehow seemed to have managed to have grown quite fat. The pigs appeared to have free run of everywhere, and as two trotted by it was just as though the two were off for a constitutional walk.

Somewhere close by dogs were barking as she followed her smiling guide into a house that had no furniture of any kind, nor windows, but had natural light from the doorway. It was here where her hostess invited her to sit on the floor, and where, in next to no time, she was invited to share a meal.

It seemed to Delfi that the thin lady could barely afford to feed herself, but she was so fearful of offending her pride that she smiled, and took the bowl of rice that was offered.

Later that afternoon, her hostess took her for a walk around the village where shy but smiling children walked with them. They had just left a ridge that looked out over a beautiful panorama when, on turning about, Delfi spotted Boden and the headman coming up the hill towards them, and suddenly her heart started to beat erratically.

'We'd better think about getting back,' Boden stated as he halted and she neared him. 'Ready?' he asked.

Delfi told him she was, and turned to sincerely thank her hostess, who walked back to the Land Rover with them, where Boden thanked the headman for his hospitality, and with the children smiling sunnily, and waving enthusiastically, they left the village.

'Well?' Boden enquired amicably as they bumped over impossible tracks.

'Very,' Delfi replied, and given that she spoke not a word of her hostess's language, nor her hostess hers, she just the same felt that they had communicated quite happily, and told him truthfully, 'I enjoyed it very much.'

He made no comment, but as Delfi hung on to the holding-bar, and Boden did his best to avoid bone-breaking hazards, a couple of hours later they arrived back at their not so primitive accommodation in what Delfi believed was mutual harmony.

She felt sorely in need of a shower by that time and parted from Boden to go to her apartment to shower and to dream and to hope that—maybe—Boden would take her with him again before his work here was completed.

She dressed and brushed her hair, and wished most fervently that she were at the start of her working assignment rather than coming to the end. By quick calculation, she reckoned that she had little more than a week left of being with him. It was not long enough.

Delfi closed her mind to the dark thought that once it was over she would never see him again. Instead, she decided she would make the most of the time she had left to store up precious memories. To that end, on hearing Boden leaving his apartment and enter the sitting-room, even though it was much earlier than usual, she left hers.

'It seems we're both eager for dinner.' He smiled charmingly as she joined him, and, while her heart set up a crazy rhythm just to have him continue to be pleasant to her, he asked, 'How do you feel about getting some work out of the way while we're waiting for Seri?'

'Seems like a good idea,' she agreed, and spent the next hour being amazed at how much of the still-maintained customs and traditions Boden had gleaned from the headman of the hill tribe they had visited that day.

Dinner, when it arrived, was another of Seri's mother's specialities, *nua pad namman hoi*, which was beef with oyster sauce and green vegetables. Delfi realised that she was famished, and tucked in heartily—quite unaware that Boden had been watching her until, suddenly, he spoke.

'I never thought, when first I saw you, slim, proud, and too beautiful to consider enduring any of life's hardships,' he remarked, 'that I'd one day soon share a meal with you in such rudimentary surroundings—and that you'd actually *enjoy* it!'

Delfi loved his 'too beautiful' but, while she hid that her heart was pounding deafeningly away, she raised laughing eyes to his, and told him impudently, 'That's the trouble with you sophisticated types—you think you know it all!'

It was pure bliss when he tipped back his head and a roar of laughter left him. 'I'll get you for that,' he promised with a grin.

Boden, oh, Boden, Delfi thought, and swiftly turned
her eyes back down to her plate. She felt like putty to
the core about him, and loved him more then than at
any time since she had known of her true feelings for
him. Even so, as the meal ended and Seri came in to
clear the table and then went away again, she began to
grow agitated. Boden had remained in a good humour
throughout, but—was her enjoyment showing *too much*?

Panic assaulted her full-square at that thought. Boden
had observed that she had pride, and she felt then that
she'd die of embarrassment if, from her present attitude, he so much as caught a glimpse of how very much
she cared for him.

Abruptly, she stood up. Boden was as sharp as a tack,
and much though she wanted to stay in the same room
with him she was going to pieces fast and was too
churned up inside to risk it.

He was on his feet too, and was quite close when,
turning away, she stated, 'I think I'll call it a day!' She
then immediately, agitatedly, realised that he might have
more dictation for her. 'That is, if you've nothing...'
Her voice broke off when, not knowing that he had
moved, she turned back again, and somehow bumped
into him.

'Don't...' he began at the same time, but as they col-
lided what else he'd been about to say all at once got
lost.

Delfi was lost too from just the feel of the tall strength
of him touching her. She was lost totally, and was staring
at him wide-eyed and mesmerised when, involuntarily it
seemed, his right hand came up and he tenderly stroked
his forefinger down the side of her face.

'Delfi,' he breathed, and gently he kissed her.

It seemed then by unspoken mutual consent that they
went into each other's arms. Delfi certainly had no ob-

jection to make when, with his arms firm about her, Boden once more lowered his head, and kissed her again.

Her arms tightened about him and they shared kiss after kiss. She was clinging on to him tightly, her body pressed up against his, when he trailed tender, gentle kisses down her throat and then back up to her left ear.

She wasn't thinking at all, but merely feeling and adoring, when suddenly his arms about her went rigid, and he stilled. In the next moment he was pulling back from her, his voice harsh as he grated, 'You still think you're in love with your sister's man?'

She sucked in a swift breath of shock, and came rapidly back to earth. It seemed light years away that she had ever imagined herself in love with Hugh Renshaw, but whatever happened she was going to guard against Boden's knowing that—or knowing where her love really did lie.

She was still feeling all over the place, however, when she hurriedly pushed at Boden and took a step back. Instinctive pride alone was working for her. 'I don't have to *think* what my feelings are for Hugh Renshaw,' she fired while she still could, 'I *know*!'

Staring proudly up at him, Delfi did not miss the clench of Boden's jaw as she unrepentantly brought out Hugh's name. 'You love him?' he insisted grimly.

'You can't turn love off like a tap!' she snapped, and wanted to be in her own room away from the disgust she knew she would soon see in Boden's eyes.

To her utter astonishment, though, it was not disgust she saw in his eyes but, as he caught a hold of her by her upper arms, absolute fury as he roared, 'So you've just been *using* me to forget *him*!'

It was the very last thing Delfi would have thought of doing, but she was just desperate enough then to latch on to any suggestion—even if she did have to lower her eyes to do it when, lying through her teeth, she replied, 'I'm human enough to—to be able to respond—without love being there.'

'So you *were* using me!' he snarled, and the next Delfi knew he had in one enraged movement picked her up in his arms. He did not put her down again until they were in her room, the place he chose to set her down—her bed.

With energy born of sudden fear, Delfi went to rocket from the bed. But, moving fast for a man of his height, he had caught her before she had moved half a step— and had found a very expedient way of preventing her from going anywhere.

'Let me up!' Delfi yelled on discovering that instead of being vertical she was now horizontal on her mattress and that Boden was anchoring her down with his body.

'When I'm ready,' he raged, and in the next moment his face was closer to hers; a moment later his lips had claimed hers.

'No!' she protested when she had breath, but it was a feeble protest, for Boden's mouth was over hers again, and a weakness was invading her. A weakness that, when she knew full well she should be fighting him to the bitter end, was making a nonsense of any such reasoning. 'No!' she again protested the next time her lips were free, but her protest was so faint it was barely audible and, when Boden took her lips again, this time, as if of their own volition, her arms went up and around him.

She was soon lost to everything save him and her need for him, and when he pressed his body down against hers she pressed up to meet him. I love you, she wanted to tell him, but her lips were in his keeping again.

How she came to be semi-naked she neither knew nor cared as Boden took her to an enchanted land, making her rapturous with delight when his gentle fingers teased and caressed the naked globes of her breasts, and he kissed and moulded the pink tormented tips.

Take me, she wanted to cry when with his hands on her hips he pulled her yet closer to him. His mouth was at her throat, his lips moving up to the back of her ear when, 'All right?' he questioned gently.

Delfi was in a no man's land of wanting and could only think that he was asking if it was all right that they made love—totally. And, 'Oh—yes,' she breathed shyly, and held on to him tightly when, not wanting any mis-understanding, not at this late stage, 'I want you. I want you so much,' she confessed urgently. And then, instead of being loved totally—was totally shocked.

One moment she and Boden were pressed so close together on the bed it would have been impossible to get anything between them—and, the next, there was not only space between their two bodies, but he wasn't even on the bed.

'What...?' she questioned, feeling completely bewildered that, when she had just verbally assented to the removal of any barrier Boden might have thought was there to prevent his taking her, he had suddenly sprung away from her.

'What indeed?' he drawled, his tone alone like a douche of cold water to her inflamed senses, before he went on, 'This is where you learn, sweetheart, that nobody uses *me* like *that*!'

Delfi was still trying to make sense of what he was saying when with a slam of finality the door crashed to after him. Then the other door closed as angrily; he went out into the night. It didn't take her long after that to come down from the dizzy heights he had taken her to, to realise that he wasn't coming back. A minute later and she'd realised that what he'd meant by his 'nobody uses *me* like *that*' was that he would never countenance being used as a substitute for anyone. Clearly, he thought that she was using him as a substitute for Hugh. Oh, if only he knew.

Delfi spent a dreadful night, going over and over everything in her mind, while at the same time she listened for the sound of Boden returning. But he did not come back and by morning she had hit rock-bottom.

Then suddenly, as she heard the sound of a footfall outside, her heartbeats quickened. The next sound she heard, however, was that of the Land Rover being started up and being driven away—and Delfi discovered that it was possible to sink lower than rock-bottom. Boden must be so disgusted at her behaviour, so contemptuous of what he thought were her standards, that he preferred to do without breakfast rather than risk seeing her more than he had to.

Delfi faced the fact that she was not in a position to tell him differently—that she had not been thinking of Hugh when he had been making love to her—and knew at that moment that there was nothing she could do but leave. It was certain that she could not go on like this.

Delfi left Thailand without seeing Boden again. She was still in a stunned kind of shock when the plane she'd managed to catch landed in Delhi, stayed for forty-five minutes, and then took off again.

Thoughts of Boden were still spinning around in her head when the Thai International flight landed at Heathrow. Delfi was by then beginning to think that she would never be free of him.

Hang the expense, she thought despondently, and taking a taxi sat thinking of how Boden would know by now that she had walked out on the job. She hadn't left him a note—she hardly thought a note necessary. Should he bother to ask questions though—after running up the flag on finding she'd departed, that was—then Seri would doubtless tell him how he'd given her a lift on the back of his motorbike to Chiang Rai airport.

Delfi had a brief respite from having Boden so constantly in her head when she recalled how she'd gone looking for Seri the moment she'd decided to leave. She had asked if he could give her a lift into the nearest town, but when she had told him that she intended to fly home to England, 'I'll take you to the airport,' he'd insisted proudly. Not only that, but, when she'd been desperate enough not to mind leaving her large case behind, he'd insisted also that her luggage would be no problem. That was when Delfi had remembered one day seeing him laden to full capacity with provisions—she'd believed him. Luck had been with her every step of the way after that. She'd been lucky in getting a flight straight away from Chiang Rai to Bangkok and, because of a plane delay in Bangkok, she'd been lucky enough to catch a flight to England.

There had been many times on that journey when Delfi had had to fight a battle against tears. And, as the taxi turned into the close where she lived, and where everything was dearly familiar, she was again having to push back tears.

'*Delfi!*' her mother exclaimed in delighted surprise when she came out into the hall to see who it was who was letting themselves into her home.

'Hello, Mum,' Delfi smiled, and was warmly hugged and made a fuss of for the next ten minutes until they adjourned to the sitting-room with a pot of coffee.

'Why didn't you let me know you were coming? I'd have met you at the airport,' her mother declared, as she studied the shadows under her daughter's eyes that told their own tale.

'I—er—sort of left in a hurry,' Delfi replied, wanting to fib a little but, as ever, having tremendous difficulty when it came to lying to her mother.

'Oh...?' her mother queried. And, when Delfi wasn't very forthcoming, 'Did Melvin Dalloway prove—troublesome?' Delfi stared at her, having not given Mel Dalloway a thought in an age. Then all at once her mother was discounting that idea and appeared to have hit on another reason when she brought out the name of another man who hadn't featured too much in Delfi's thinking of late either. 'If you've come home because you can't bear to be parted from Hugh Renshaw, then Raina won't stand in your way,' she told her solemnly, adding, 'Raina's broken off their engagement.'

'Br...?' Delfi was having a hard time taking it in. She had gone away because of her imagined love for Hugh and had intended to stay away for a year. She had returned with eleven months to go having not given a thought to the problem of Hugh—simply because, to her, he was no longer a problem. 'You say Raina's engagement's off?' she questioned in a sudden hurry as the implications of that all at once hit her. 'She's all right?' she went on anxiously. 'She's not ill, like she was——?'

'She's fine, absolutely fine,' her mother smiled. And was still smiling as she reminded Delfi, 'It was *Raina* who broke the engagement, not Hugh.'

'But why?' she pressed, as guilt began to gnaw away.

'Apparently Raina realised that she didn't love him.'

'Didn't...doesn't?'

'Neither,' her mother laughed, and confided, 'It seems that a certain Lawrence Bolt joined her firm some four months ago. Your sister fell in love—truly in love—with him at first sight, but because of her previous unhappy experience of a broken engagement fought against it.

Unbeknown to her, it was a mutual falling in love at first sight, but since she was wearing another man's ring Lawrence decided to look for another job. Before he gave his notice in, though, he sought Raina out and pointedly asked her how she would feel if she never saw him again.'

A knife twisted in Delfi that she would never see Boden again, and it took her all she had to keep her pain from showing. 'What did Raina say?' she asked.

'I don't think she had to say anything. But she must have looked pretty devastated at the thought— Lawrence took it from there.'

'They're engaged?' she asked, hiding her own devastation.

Her mother shook her head. 'Lawrence says he'll give her diamonds after they're married. In his view two engagements are enough for any woman—he wants to put a wedding band on her finger first.'

'Isn't that lovely?' Delfi whispered.

'It is,' her mother agreed, quite obviously approving of Lawrence. 'Now,' she said encouragingly, 'how about you?'

To Delfi it seemed that what her parent was asking was how about her and Hugh Renshaw. 'Like Raina,' she told her mother openly, 'I've discovered that I don't love Hugh, after all.'

For long seconds the mother who knew her so well just sat and looked at her. Then, 'And, like Raina, you too have found out what true love really does feel like, haven't you?'

Delfi opened her mouth to deny it, but then found that she could not. 'Does it show?' she asked unhappily.

'He—doesn't—return your feelings?' her mother questioned, treading carefully.

'No,' Delfi replied briefly, a knife twisting again as cold reality hit home that Boden did not even like her, let alone love her.

'Where is he?'

'Still in Thailand,' Delfi replied.

'Not—Melvin Dalloway?'

'Never Mel Dalloway,' Delfi told her.

'It hurts, and I'm prying too much, aren't I, darling?' her mother said gently, and looked near to tears herself a moment before she suddenly smiled, and said bracingly, 'You look as though you could sleep for a week—you must be jet-lagged. Why not go up to bed for a couple of hours?'

Delfi went up to her old bedroom wishing that all that was wrong with her was jet lag. She owned that she was out on her feet, however, so wasn't totally surprised that she went spark out for a couple of hours shortly after her head touched the pillows.

She was up again, bathed and dressed, by the time her sister returned home from work. 'You're back!' Raina declared gleefully, and having hugged each other, 'Thank goodness you're home,' she beamed. 'I'm getting married in March; I'll need you here for your bridesmaid dress fittings.'

'Mother tells me you love another,' Delfi laughed— and was amazed at her sister's reply.

'By the sound of it, you're over the crush you had on Hugh.'

'You knew about it?' Delfi gasped.

'Was it very painful?' Raina asked gently. 'I wanted to try and help you, to talk to you about it, but I was afraid, loving Lawrence as I did, that I might end up pushing you at Hugh—for all the wrong reasons.'

'Dope!' Delfi scorned, glad Raina had said nothing to her—it had taken Boden, knowing Boden, to show her that a 'crush' was indeed all that she had felt for Hugh. 'So,' she said brightly, 'when do I get to meet this Lawrence?'

Instantly, Raina forgot all about Hugh. 'Tonight,' she answered dreamily. Then their father arrived home.

'Well, hello, stranger!' He grinned his delight, and added drily, 'Thanks for letting us know you were coming.'

'Oh, Dad!' Delfi cried self-defensively.

'I'll forgive you,' he teased. 'Come and give your old Dad a kiss.'

Delfi went to bed that night having met Lawrence Bolt, a quiet, unassuming man, whose eyes followed her sister everywhere. It was plain that Raina and Lawrence were happy just to be in each other's company, and Delfi felt happy for them.

She got up the next morning and, with Boden having taken up permanent residence in her head, realised that the sooner she got herself something to keep her busy the better.

To that end she scanned the situations vacant column in the paper, and spotted a job that was easily within her capabilities, and which, by the wording, sounded as if they wanted a secretary who could start pretty well straight away.

That, she decided, couldn't be better, and she telephoned at once for an interview. 'I've an appointment with a Mr Halliday at twelve tomorrow,' she told her mother as she put down the phone.

'If that's what you want, dear,' her mother smiled, and earned more of Delfi's gratitude that instead of saying the 'You could get a much better job than that' which she was sure she was thinking, she opted to change the subject. 'Now are you sure you don't want to come with me to the Guild luncheon today?'

'Positive,' Delfi declared. 'You go off and be waited on for a change.'

Half an hour after her mother had gone Delfi was starting to regret that she had not gone with her. She was upstairs in her room ostensibly emptying yesterday's suitcase prior to putting it away. The only problem there was that, in unpacking, she came across the trousers and T-shirts, the 'uniform' which Boden had bought her and, as he again took possession of her head, all unpacking ceased.

An hour later, she was still in her room and was making a concentrated effort to get herself back to the Delfi Washington she was when anyone else was around when the front doorbell pealed.

She felt relieved to have company other than her own and Boden, her silent, unseen, but disapproving companion, and she raced downstairs ready, should it be some vacuum cleaner salesman, to invite him in to demonstrate his wares.

To her surprise, though—not to say horror—the person who stood there when she had the door open was not a salesman, but Hugh Renshaw!

'Oh—er—hello, Hugh,' she managed brightly enough, while at the same time—and with a certain degree of shame—unable to help wondering how on *earth* she had ever imagined herself in love with him. 'Er—Raina isn't in,' she told him, while her heart beat regularly and she noted that not only did Hugh look nothing like her beloved Boden, he wasn't, and never would be, in the same street.

'Now what makes you think I've come to see Raina?' Hugh questioned, with what at one time she might have thought was an engaging smile, but which now only drew her attention to the weakness of his mouth. 'I asked for an extended lunch hour the minute I knew you were back,' he stated and, uninvited, stepped over the threshold.

'News—um—travels fast,' Delfi commented lightly, but took a hurried pace backwards when he made a grab for her.

'So did I,' Hugh leered, 'when Nick Jackson told me at the office this morning that he'd spotted you at Heathrow yesterday.'

Nick Jackson, she vaguely remembered, had been at a party a crowd of them, including Raina and Hugh, had gone to ages ago. 'It's—a small world,' she trotted out tritely as she took another rapid pace backwards when Hugh lunged towards her.

'It never was big enough to keep you and me apart!' he told her, and before she could stop him he had grabbed hold of her. Delfi remembered, as he fastened his weak mouth over hers, how he had once questioned how she could let one man kiss her while she was in love with another, and as nausea and anger attacked she pushed at him with all her might. She was in love with Boden. She didn't want any man's kisses but his; any other man's lips were entirely revolting.

'I don't love you!' she told Hugh angrily as she forced him to break his hold on her. And, as she recalled how he'd been forever trying to make a grab for her during the time he must have been kissing Raina, 'Nor do you love me,' she told him.

That, she was to discover, was a mistake, because Hugh spent the next ten minutes in trying to alternately make a grab for her and convince her that he did love her.

'I'm sorry, Hugh,' she was forced to tell him in the end, 'I just—don't want your love.'

'How can you say that? You were as hot as hell for me at one time!' he accused nastily.

From what Delfi could remember of it, they had shared several kisses, but only one mutual embrace—but if he wanted to believe that made her 'as hot as hell' for him, he was welcome. She was in fact growing rather weary of the whole business.

'Whatever I was, I am not now!' she told him crossly, and, certain whatever his protestations that he did not love her, 'So, I'd——'

'You're only saying that because of Raina.'

'No, I'm not,' Delfi replied, and, because she could see that there was no other way of convincing him, she told him, 'I've met someone else.'

'You're... you're saying you love somebody else?'

Delfi took a deep breath. 'That's what I'm saying,' she agreed, but would not deny her love for Boden when for the next few minutes Hugh insisted that she could not possibly love anyone but him. Then he spent the following few minutes haranguing her and, starting to feel sorry for himself, wheedling and trying to play on her sympathies. Then finally, when all Delfi felt was dreadfully uncomfortable, he gave up acting, and, his true self coming to the fore, he ended up swearing, and having called her a few awful names strutted off down the path as though well pleased with himself.

Delfi returned upstairs after he'd gone, convinced of one thing above all others from his visit: Hugh Renshaw had never loved her, nor indeed anyone but Hugh Renshaw. Certain of that, Delfi could only be heartily glad that her sister was not going to marry him. My heavens, had Raina had a lucky escape!

Delfi was nevertheless still feeling shaken by what had taken place when she heard her mother's car pull on to the drive. Only then did Delfi realise that, since her mother's car was invariably parked on the drive, by its absence Hugh must have worked out that her mother was out, and that, if in, then her younger daughter would be in alone.

It was perhaps because she was still feeling shaken to have seen the 'other side' of Hugh Renshaw that Delfi kept the fact of his lunchtime visit to herself. She did not want the other members of her family to be upset, and spent a pleasant evening with them, before going up to bed to have not Hugh in her head, but a man who was a man—Boden.

She then tried to pin her thoughts on her job interview tomorrow. But that only brought on thoughts of how she had not behaved very well in running out on the job she'd had with Boden. Though, as she strove for some stiffening, she decided that his behaviour hadn't been exactly saintly, had it?

Any stiffening she'd garnered fell apart at the seams, however, when it suddenly dawned on her that, having been paid for a month's work by Boden, and having worked for only three weeks, she owed him some money.

Delfi got up the next morning wondering if she should look up his business address and send him a cheque for the amount which she had walked off with, but had never earned.

'Best of luck with your interview,' her mother smiled as she waved her off.

'Thanks, Mum,' Delfi smiled back, her thoughts not on her job interview, but taken up with trying to assess honestly which she should do for the best. Would it be better to forget about the money she owed him—was she not in any case perhaps in some Freudian way merely wanting to keep in touch with him, by making some contact with him? It couldn't be that, could it? She owed him the money, so surely it had to be better that she posted a cheque to his office so that it would be there waiting when he returned from Thailand next week?

Delfi was still cogitating that the latter seemed to be by far the most businesslike thing to do when she walked in to her noontime job appointment with Mr Halliday, sailed through the interview, and went back home again.

She knew, as she turned into the close where she lived, that she should be a little thrilled at least that she had a job she was due to start on Monday, but she was too busy in pondering whether she should after all learn to live with her conscience and forget all about the money she owed Boden.

That way, anyhow, she'd know for sure that it wasn't her love for him that was pulling the strings of her actions. There was the last word in classy cars parked outside her house when she got there. She ignored it; daytime parking anywhere in that area was a nightmare—everyone parked where they could.

Delfi pinned a smile on her face as she went through the garden gate and up to her front door. She let herself into the hall, and was about to find some enthusiasm with which to tell her mother about her interview when her mother appeared from nowhere, and, looking a little flustered, instead of asking her how she'd got on whispered, 'You've a visitor!'

'A visitor?' Delfi blinked, but even while she was taking in that something very much out of the ordinary, not to say stupendous, must be happening to cause her mother to look in any way flustered her parent was urging her along the hall.

'I've been entertaining him in the sitting-room for you,' she told her, and suddenly Delfi was realising that by entertaining 'him' Hugh Renshaw must have taken another extended lunch hour.

'Mum, I . . .' Delfi started to protest, and, as she belatedly wished now that she'd said something about

Hugh's visit yesterday, they reached the sitting-room door.

But, even while Delfi was realising that her mother could not after all have believed her when she'd told her that she'd discovered that she didn't love Hugh, her mother was reaching down to the door-handle and was opening it and was urging her through.

Inwardly Delfi sighed. Hugh must have come for a repeat performance of yesterday. She felt more than a little fed up at that prospect, and decided that she would keep the sitting-room door open. No matter what romantic notions her mother must be nursing about her and Hugh Renshaw, she knew she would stand no nonsense should he start to loudly swear and harangue her as he'd done yesterday.

'Mum...' she tried to warn her.

'I've some jobs to do in the kitchen,' her parent smiled, and walked away kitchenwards.

Delfi looked after her for a moment, then, squaring her shoulders for battle, she stepped into the sitting-room. And then, as her heart began to race, she stopped dead while still at the sitting-room door.

A man, a man much taller than Hugh Renshaw, was standing by the window. He moved, came nearer, his blue-green eyes fixed firmly on her face. She had forgotten how tanned he was but not how virile, how manly, how wonderful, how absolutely *everything*, he was.

'Boden!' she gasped, and when he halted halfway across the carpet she, without thinking, while staring disbelievingly at him, closed the sitting-room door.

CHAPTER EIGHT

MORE from a need to have some moments to get herself together than anything else, Delfi came away from the door and, while trying desperately hard to keep her expression cool, she moved further into the room.

'I—er—didn't...' Her voice tailed off as she fought panic from the sudden thought that her mother must have guessed that Boden was the man she loved and was trying to help her. 'I thought you weren't due back until next week,' she went on evenly, realising that what she must do at all costs was to prevent *Boden* from guessing how she felt about him. With that in mind, she assumed an air of being more in control than she was, and held out her right hand.

Boden, with an unfathomable glint suddenly there in his blue-green eyes, ignored her outstretched hand. Delfi couldn't have said that she was truly sorry. Perhaps, knowing what his touch to her skin could do to her, she had been rather rash to invite him to shake hands.

'I'm surprised that you returned so early too,' he replied shortly.

Panic again smote her—she didn't want him taking any in-depth look into why she had left without giving him the courtesy of a farewell. 'I owe you some money,' she blurted out, and saw that he seemed irritated by her remark. That pleased her; at least it had taken his mind off *why* she had left.

It was her turn to be irritated, though, when, just as though the house were his, 'Take a seat,' he suggested shortly.

About to remind him that his name didn't feature anywhere in the deeds to the property, Delfi then started to get a reaction from seeing him so unexpectedly, and, as her legs suddenly went like jelly, she experienced a most definite need to sit down.

On either side of the fireplace two settees were positioned opposite each other. She opted for the one furthest away from him, and felt marginally better when, with a curt flicked glance to her, Boden went over to the other one.

They were sitting facing each other, and that glint was still there in his eyes, she saw. But that was when, hoping he would go, hoping he would stay, feeling mixed up and extremely on edge, Delfi found that good manners, instilled in her over the years, came in as a tremendous help.

'Has my mother offered you coffee?' she enquired politely—and had to weather his acid look that plainly said he wasn't too thrilled with her attitude.

He had an ample store of good manners too, though, she found when, his voice courteous, even, he replied, 'Your mother was kind enough to offer me lunch.' Oh, grief— Delfi started to become agitated again— Boden could be with them for another hour. 'But,' he added, 'I declined.'

Immediately she wanted that extra hour with him. 'I expect you're extremely busy,' she murmured off the top of her head, and, as it came to her that he must have an appointment near by and because he was so close must have decided to call in to tear her off a strip for running out on the job, another thought struck her. 'How did you find out where I lived?' she enquired.

'Finding out where you live was the least of my problems!' he answered shortly, and, before she could begin to wonder what other problems he had, to her amazement, and still in that same short tone, he demanded, 'How many sisters do you have?'

'Er—just the one—Raina,' Delfi was surprised enough to respond. She saw him frown, and would have loved to have known what was going on behind his high intelligent forehead. Most definitely, her answer had not pleased him.

'Your mother tells me that Raina is to marry in March,' he remarked. Then, looking straight at her, his blue-green eyes were suddenly piercing hers. 'A man called Lawrence,' he stated succinctly.

'That's right,' Delfi agreed, a whole cartload of nerves spiking her. 'We're all very pl——'

'You told me her fiancé's name was Hugh—Hugh Renshaw!' Boden charged, his chin jutting at an aggressive angle—but his eyes never leaving her face.

Delfi blinked, and would have given anything to know why Boden was taking issue with her on the subject. Nobody liked being lied to, it was true, but . . . 'I wasn't lying,' she followed her own train of thought. 'Hugh was her fiancé, but she—um—fell out of love with him, and in love with Lawrence.'

Barely had the words left her when, to her further amazement, Boden turned on her in one mighty fury, and, 'Which you think leaves the field clear for you?' he slammed the question at her.

'I don't want him!' she erupted, with more heat than thought.

She had time to reflect on her too swift reply, when, although his fury was fading fast, Boden seemed to need a moment to gather some control. There was a watchful look about him, though, when after some moments of just sitting and looking consideringly at her he drawled, 'Poor Renshaw. You and your sister both fell out of love with him.'

'I...' Helplessly Delfi searched for words. She wanted Boden away from the subject of love—didn't fully know how they'd got on to the subject—but could only feel fear while they were in that area. But, more particularly at that moment, she badly needed a smoke-screen. She thought she found one when she coolly stated, 'A woman has her pride,' and even managed an aloof trace of a smile as, 'I draw the line at having anybody's cast-offs— even my sister's.' She recalled only then that Boden, that very first day when he'd taken her to a hotel in Bangkok, had said almost the selfsame thing.

That watchful look was still in his eyes, however, but if he was remembering it too, he did not refer to it, but, to cause her fresh alarm, 'But how can Renshaw be considered a cast-off?' he enquired in a voice that was almost silky. 'He'd declared his love for you *before* your sister had bidden him a final adieu, hadn't he?'

Desperately Delfi wished she could remember all that she'd revealed to Boden about her love for Hugh and Hugh's love for her. But with panic, a fair degree of confusion, warning bells constantly going off in her head, and everything else, she was having enough difficulty in coping with the here and now, without delving too deeply into the past.

'Yes...but——' she tried.

'You could have taken him from your sister while he was engaged to her.' Boden was giving her no time to get her head together.

She had never forgotten how disgusted he had been by her behaviour over her sister's fiancé. 'That—er— was the impression he gave me,' she admitted, but then found that because she loved Boden so she still wanted him to think well of her. 'But I couldn't,' she tacked on rapidly, 'not without hurting Raina.'

'So why not now?' he asked, causing her to realise, too late, that in seeking his approbation she had spoken much too rapidly, much too without proper thought. 'Now that she's planning to wed someone else in March, she would only be glad surely, not hurt, by your taking Renshaw?'

'I . . .' she began, and floundered abysmally. And that was when, her only defence stripped from her, she did the only thing left to her—she came out fighting. 'Look here, Boden, none of this has anything to do with why you're here!' she attacked shortly, rushing on, 'I didn't expect you to come to my home after . . .' As a wayward memory of being in his arms returned, she stumbled, but swiftly picked herself up and, trying to oust the memory of how Boden had deliberately started to make love to her—only to reject her—she charged on, 'But I'll accept I should have left you a note perhaps, or— left some of the money you paid m—— '

'You've seen him? You've seen him since you came home?' he cut her off thunderously.

Delfi stared at him in astonishment. It was just as if, so set on keeping to the one track, he simply hadn't heard a word she was saying! *'Who?'* she snapped belligerently.

'Renshaw—who else?' he rapped toughly.

Her jaw dropped, but a moment later she was replying spiritedly, 'If you *must* know—yes, I have! But that's——'

'What did he want?'

Really! Was there no end to his cheek? She'd taken a haranguing from Hugh Renshaw yesterday. But Boden McLaine or no Boden McLaine, she wasn't taking another one today. 'What *would* he want?' she fired.

'You?' he interrogated grimly. Stubbornly, she refused to answer. 'But you told him "no"?' She kept her lips firmly sealed. 'Why?' Boden insisted on getting a reply.

Delfi stood up. He stood up too—and took a step nearer. She counted ten, a very shaky ten, she admitted and, having gained a little control, thought it was time to change the subject.

'Have you seen your father since you returned?' she trotted out, hoping that by turning to the door Boden might take the hint and do likewise.

She took a step forward, but had barely moved in that direction when Boden caught a firm hold of her upper arm and prevented her from moving any further. 'My father is not one of my priorities right now!' he retorted grittily, and as her heart raced out of control at his touch he swung her round to face him, and looking coldly down into her wide violet eyes, 'Why?' he questioned determinedly.

Trying her hardest to cope with first things first, Delfi pulled her arm out of his hold. To her relief, he let go. 'Why do I ask?' she queried, starting to feel marginally better—even though he was now standing much closer to her than he had been.

'Why "no"—to Renshaw?' he barked, clearly impatient with her. Delfi gave him a withering look—it bounced off him, when, hell-bent on being answered it seemed, he demanded, *'Well?'*

'Well nothing!' she exploded—if he wasn't taking kindly to her attitude, and was impatient of it, well, that went double for her. 'Why the questioning—why c-come here to my home? Why——?'

'You're hedging!' he sliced in accusingly. Then, as if his sharp brain was jetting to delve into why that should be, suddenly he was leaning back on his heels and seemed to be studying every expression, every nuance, that crossed her face. Then, while she was starting to become a mass of inner agitation, 'You're nervous!' he all at once declared. And, as Delfi tried to find her voice to tell him how wrong his surmise was, 'Why are you nervous?' he wanted to know. But his tone was changing—his aggressiveness seeming to abate a trifle. Then suddenly, as he continued to observe her, he was all calm, all reasoning, when, quietly, he questioned, 'What is it that you're so nervous of, Delfi?'

'Nothing! I'm not!' she blurted in a rapid burst of frightened energy. She had been panic-stricken to start with, and look how quickly he had drawn the conclusion he had! No wonder she was nervous! He had shown his tenacity by refusing to leave off his questioning about Hugh. What else might he conclude, if she couldn't stop him?

But, for the moment, her thinking processes seemed locked in stunned 'hold', and although she was aware of Boden's quiet, studying gaze on her she could not find a self-protective word to say.

Strangely then, though, while all she wanted to do was to run and hide, Boden, after a moment more of looking directly at her, looked briefly away, then took what seemed oddly to be a steadying breath. Then, to her utter astoundment, he all at once queried, 'Would it help, in any way, should I confess that I'm feeling not a little apprehensive—nervous—myself at this moment?'

Her wide violet eyes went huge. Boden apprehensive? Nervous? Never! She hesitated—to her knowledge he was not a liar and, as he stood looking levelly at her, she could see no reason why he should start to lie now. 'You...!' she gasped, with what voice shock had left her.

Boden did not repeat what he had said. Instead he again took a hold of her arm and, while she was still shaken by his confession, he led her to the nearest settee.

They were seated on the two-seater settee together by the time that Delfi had got her wits back. She was grateful therefore that, while she coped with the fact that again Boden was much closer to her than he had been, he let go the hold he had on her arm.

She wasn't sure then whether to aim for an aloof note or a mocking one, but found that having stirred herself to say anything at all her, 'What have *you* got to be nervous about?' fell somewhere between the two.

'I'm encouraged,' he replied slowly after a second, 'that within what you've just said lies an admission that you are in fact nervous about something yourself.' Delfi tried hard for an uppity look—he was too clever by half—but suddenly found that she could look how she pleased, but he was intent on looking beyond the surface. And that worried her. She didn't want him looking deeper—deeper than the front she was trying to put up. 'However,' he went on when, since he was so clever she didn't want him sifting through anything else she might say, she stayed silent, 'it seems to fall on me; that is, it seems I'm going to have to explain—hmm—some of my—behaviour.'

'Your—behaviour?' she questioned haltingly, with no idea of what was coming now.

His eyes were fixed on hers when he owned, 'Behaviour that seemed to *me* to be irrational a good deal of the time. So lord knows what you made of it.'

'Oh...?' she queried, doing her utmost to keep her curiosity under control but, because he was Boden, failing miserably.

'I'm not normally a short-tempered edgy brute,' he stated evenly.

'You could have fooled me!' she found a stray wisp of spirit to instantly retort.

'One way and another, there's been a lot of "fooling" going on,' he replied. Delfi, who was doing her best to 'fool' him about her innermost feelings, decided it was a good moment to go on the attack again.

'You were short-tempered with me from the moment you met me at Bangkok airport!' she found another strand of spirit to retort tartly, and was made to endure more of his long steady scrutiny.

Then, with just the vaguest trace of a smile about his well-shaped mouth, he revealed, 'I realised, only a short while ago, that if I'm to stand any chance at all of—achieving—all I want to achieve—at whatever cost to myself—then I must be totally honest with you, Delfi.' And, as she stared at him with some fair degree of mystification, all hint of a smile left him, and, 'That being so, I have to admit that I was very much anti-Adelfia Washington before I'd so much as clapped eyes on you.'

'Thanks!' she sniffed, vulnerable in her love for him and wide open to hurt from even the smallest slight.

'It's not my intention to offend you,' he swiftly stated.

'Merely to be honest,' Delfi countered, quickly realising that to argue aloofly that he hadn't caused her offence would bring more attention to her hurt than she wanted.

'To be honest,' he agreed, and, after giving her another of his steady straight looks, he resumed, 'I'd given my father my word that I'd whip round to the arrivals area to meet you, but . . .' He paused, then went on, 'I'll apologise in advance, but—to be honest— I was more interested in getting to the exhibition than in messing about meeting what sounded like some man's floozie off a plane.'

'Floozie!' she erupted. 'I wonder you bothered!'

'I'd given my word,' he weathered her acid to remind her. 'With my father being in a rushed state about getting home to Gina— I couldn't do anything other. Though as far as I was concerned, once I'd dropped you off where you wanted to go, my duty would be done and I could then forget about you and concentrate on my business.' He paused for a moment, and then, looking directly into her violet eyes, he quietly added, 'But all too soon I discovered—that you are impossible to forget.'

Her heart hammered away at his look, her throat went dry at what he said, and Delfi was having a mammoth task in keeping herself all of one piece. Boden, with his looks, his words, seemed to be confessing more than he was actually saying but—she mustn't be ridiculous and read anything into nuances that just weren't there.

'Oh, of course,' she found some semblance of a brain to reply, even while she cursed that her voice was suddenly a touch husky. 'With the traffic being what it was, you were still there when I came out of the First Export and Import offices.' Her heart slowed to a sorely disappointed beat, while her head scoffed that naturally he couldn't so soon forget all about her—inside a very few minutes she had reappeared, hadn't she? He'd have had to be blind not to have noticed her.

'I was still there,' he agreed. 'But, to my intense annoyance, when I was certain you could stay there all day and it wouldn't bother me— I found that I was getting out of the car and coming over to you.'

'You were as short-tempered as the devil,' Delfi recollected.

'You weren't letting me get away with much,' he countered. 'As I recall it, even though it was plain that your reception at First Export wasn't a pleasant one, that still didn't stop your beautiful violet eyes from flashing out fire at me.' Delfi's heart started to pound ridiculously again from his calling her eyes 'beautiful'. 'I was still wondering why the hell I hadn't left you to get on with it,' he went on, that trace of a smile returning, 'when I found I was taking you to my hotel.'

'You had no ulterior motive,' she stated more than questioned.

She wished that she hadn't when his hint of a smile instantly vanished. 'Definitely not!' he declared firmly. Thanks a lot! Delfi thought, wounded again, while not wanting him to have had an ulterior motive, that he'd felt no desire to better his acquaintance—well, not until she'd clung on to him a week later when she'd found a snake in her room. 'Though while I'd no ulterior motive, and with you looking ready to part my hair with something exceedingly sharp, I couldn't then understand why, having booked you into my hotel—and for the same mystifying reason suggested we'd dine together—I should then set about making enquiries about your friend Dalloway.'

Delfi refrained from telling Boden that almost until the very last moment she'd had no intention of dining with him that night. But, now that they were well away from Hugh Renshaw territory and the fact that she'd told Hugh 'no', she felt less anxious, and more ready to hold her own in this conversation. Even if it was more than somewhat obscure why they were having this conversation at all.

'You discovered that he was married.'

'And you, that night, discovered that Thai food is spicy,' he returned. 'And I, that night,' he added softly, 'discovered that you had the power to make me laugh.'

Her heart skipped a beat at his tone. She counteracted it by saying tartly, 'I must have blinked and missed it. When was it?'

For answer his mouth picked up at the corners, and—it was no good, her heart just didn't know how to behave, and skipped another beat. 'You amused me when, quite rightly, you asked if I was always so disagreeable,' he revealed. 'I was determined, of course, not to be amused by you,' he went on seriously a moment later.

'You'd taken a dislike to me on sight,' she stated flatly.

But only for her eyes to go huge when, shaking his head, he replied, 'What was slow in getting through to me because I was too pig-headed to admit it was that . . .' He broke off, paused, and then, fixing his blue-green look on her violet eyes, he added deliberately, 'I had started to be interested in you, my dear Delfi.'

'Y . . .' Her voice faded. With that 'my dear Delfi' still floating about in the air that did not surprise her. 'It—er—wasn't—um—an ulterior motive?' she tried again.

His eyes were still fixed on her saucer-wide ones, when he again shook his head. 'Only later, some while later, did I realise that my—interest—in you, was born that day outside Dalloway's offices, when, shaken, perhaps defeated, you still met my foul temper with angry, sparking eyes.'

For several witless seconds her heart thundered wildly, and she could think of nothing to say, but she made great efforts to quickly get herself together. It was music to her ears of course to know that Boden was not as indifferent to her as she had so many times believed, but a confessed 'interest' in no way constituted the love she wanted, or a fondness, or even an affection for her.

'You play your cards pretty close to your chest, McLaine,' she eventually managed to trot out lightly. But, a sucker for punishment, she discovered that she wanted more than the few crumbs he had given her. 'What shape did this—um—interest take?' she just had to ask.

His expression was unsmiling as he stared at her long and hard as though trying to read what went on in her head. Delfi was determined to give nothing away, and bore his all-seeing eyes bravely. Then Boden was telling her, 'It took the form of tripping me up when I least expected it.'

'Oh,' she murmured, and, when her curiosity was rampant, managing to make her tone only politely interested, she invited, 'For instance?'

'For instance,' he obliged, 'the very next morning.'

'I saw you at breakfast,' she remembered.

'And I, to my amazement,' he responded, 'found I was offering you a job.'

'You—hadn't thought of engaging a secretary?'

'I'd only that morning heard from my father that he wasn't coming back to do the job himself. I suppose I'd some vague notion in my head of getting myself the same battery-operated tape recorder that he'd probably have used.'

'Good—heavens!' Delfi gasped.

'So you can see how astonished I felt to actually hear myself asking the question, "Can you type?"'

'You could have told me at any time that you'd changed your mind!' Delfi felt she ought to point out.

'No way!' he stated, his good humour peering out once more. 'In no time I'd convinced myself that it was a normal instinct of my business-orientated, efficiency-minded self that I should want a secretary along.'

'But you didn't need me—not truly?'

'Truly I did,' he replied with quiet sincerity, then when he was about to add something he seemed to change his mind. A few moments later though and he was going on, 'Having, so to speak, taken you on my payroll, what of course should then be more natural than that I should be furious with you and your relaxed attitude when the very next day I rang your room, and had you paged to no avail, then saw you come into the hotel with Kevin Carroll laughing your head off?'

Kevin Carroll! She'd all but forgotten the young man from Devizes with whom she'd spent that particular day. 'You—wanted me for something special that day?' she belatedly enquired.

'Not at all,' Boden replied, and she felt he actually did seem a shade nervous when, very quietly, he—astonishingly—added, 'I was just as mad as hell, as—jealous—as hell that——'

'Jealous!' left her on a gasp of breath. A second later she was wishing that she hadn't said anything because—with anything else being just too utterly fantastic—it had to be that he had not been jealous in the sense she imagined. Quite obviously Boden, because he was her boss and was paying her for her time—although it seemed equally unlikely—was possessive, not jealous, of how she spent that time. 'You resented me enjoying my day while you'd been hard at it at the exhibition?' After her surprised 'Jealous!' Delfi tried for some common-sense perspective.

For her sins, she drew down on her head a touch of his old asperity when, 'You honestly believe I'm such a killjoy?' he demanded.

'Well, you can't mean jealous in the accepted meaning of the word!' she fired back hotly, glad of his anger—at least it resurrected some of her backbone which had been in hiding for far too long.

Any stiffening she had found, however, was lost without trace when suddenly his expression softened and, when she was not at all ready for it, he reached out and took one of her hands in his. Then, 'Why can't I, Delfi?' he asked gently.

'W...' Her heart was an agitated mass of thunderous beating. 'C-can you?' she asked in reply, her eyes fixed on his, as she searched and searched to see what he was saying, for her thinking powers seemed to be suddenly seized up.

But, 'Oh, yes,' he breathed softly, as her eyes were fixed on his, his eyes, as if he too needed to see what truth she displayed, locked on hers, 'I can.'

'Oh—Boden,' she cried tremulously as her heart gave another spurt of energy.

'It—doesn't come amiss with you—that I'm saying what I'm saying?' he questioned jerkily, but none the less earnestly—seeming to need—to need some encouragement before he went any further.

But Delfi was a churned-up accumulation of confusion and fear, with a little hope thrown in. 'I d-don't know what it is that you're saying,' she whispered, wanting desperately to know, but dreadfully afraid to give him the encouragement he appeared to be seeking because it seemed to her that she must have got it totally wrong.

For answer he took a hold of her other hand, and his grip firming on hers, 'I'm saying, my dear,' he replied, his eyes positively raking hers as he spoke, 'that, even while I didn't acknowledge to myself at the time what it was, I was as jealous as hell of that youth Carroll that he could make you laugh, while my lot seemed to be to only see the frosty side of you.'

Her jaw dropped. 'No!' she gasped.

'But yes,' he told her firmly. 'I'm saying that when I'd got no plans whatsoever for you for the following day, Kevin Carroll only had to suggest you go somewhere with him and I—to my complete astonishment—find I'm wasting no time in putting a stop to that.'

'You didn't then—have plans for us to take in a Thai culture show, or...' She broke off when he shook his head.

'Nothing was further from my mind,' he confessed. 'Of course, having covered what I considered unfathomable behaviour—by following through and taking you out the next day— I then soon discovered just how very much I was enjoying your company.'

'Really?' she asked, a breathless note there in her voice which, as Boden's hands gripped convulsively on hers, she realised must have given him quite some heart.

'Don't doubt it,' he smiled. Suddenly, though, his smile had gone. 'That was,' he qualified, 'before I became aware as we drove back to Bangkok that, while you were there with me physically, your thoughts were very far away.'

'You wanted to know what was going on inside my head,' Delfi recalled after a moment.

'For my effrontery, I got served a blow that caused me too many sleepless nights when what you didn't say added up to the fact that you'd left England over love of some man.'

Somewhere deep inside Delfi started to tremble. Boden, Boden, she wanted to beg, please, please tell me what it is that you're saying. She said nothing of the sort, however, but with what voice she could find, 'I—er—didn't know that,' she said huskily, adding, 'You did seem—um—a little cross.'

'Cross! I was furious,' he responded. 'Though even while I had no notion why the idea of your loving some man in England should make me so outraged,' he added more quietly, 'that still didn't stop me from demanding that you join me for dinner.'

'Did you—find out why you were so furious?' Good manners or no, Delfi was in such a state of suspense that she had to know in just which direction what Boden had said so far was leading.

For long moments he just sat and looked at her. Then his hands left hers and moved to her upper arms. His hands were on her like a grip of iron. 'Did I ever,' he breathed softly. 'I'll own that I've been beset by a certain stubborn refusal to see what had been staring me in the face since that day when I knew the fury of jealousy; yet at the same time I discovered that it was getting—in so short a time—such that I so couldn't bear to be parted from you I was actually ordering you to have dinner with me.'

While her heart had started racing like an express, her throat felt parched, and 'Oh?' was all that she managed to croak in query.

'Oh, indeed, dearest, dearest Delfi,' he murmured. 'I didn't realise it then. In fact, not until one certain day in the north of Thailand when, with your unbelievable hair all anyhow about your lovely face, you grinned down at me from the nape of an elephant did I know that . . .' He broke off and, to make her heart drum the faster, he leaned forward and placed a reverent kiss gently on her left cheek. When he pulled back, it was to look deeply into her eyes, and to tell her, 'I knew then, at that moment, that I, my dear, was in love with you.'

'Boden!' She wasn't certain if she'd said his name, or made any sound, as hope soared. Hope—and, if she could believe what he'd said, joy.

But suddenly the iron bands on her arms were becoming tighter than ever, and, staring at him, Delfi saw that tension was in his expression, and was all about him. 'I know I've given you hell—and it's for sure I've done nothing that could cause you to like me, let alone love me a little. But,' he broke off to pause, and to take a long-drawn breath, 'but can you give me a hint, my dear one, if there is any substance at all to the desperate hopes I've allowed myself to nurture since yesterday?'

The look of strain on him was more than she could bear, but, 'You—*do*—love me?' she just had to check.

'With my life!' he unhesitatingly replied.

'Oh, Boden!' Delfi sighed. 'I've known my feelings for you since that night when, before I knew that Seri's snake was harmless, you went over to it and picked it up—and I, in fear for your life, very nearly went into heart failure.'

'Your feelings,' he questioned, that tension grown fierce in him, 'are they love?'

'Yes...' she whispered, and it was all he waited to hear.

With a wordless cry, he gathered her into his arms, and there for long, long, ageless moments, as though from some great need, he just held her fast up against him. Then, all at once, a long-pent-up kind of a sigh left him, and then he moved back so that he could see into her eyes.

'My love!' he breathed hoarsely, and only then did he salute his lips to hers.

When that tender kiss had ended, it was Delfi who, a little shakily, sighed. 'Oh, Boden!' she whispered enchantedly.

'It's true, then?' he asked softly. 'As I love you, you love me?'

She nodded, her eyes ashine with her love for him. She had no demur to make when, as though from some desperate need—the reality of her being there with him no figment of his imagination—he again gathered her up against his heart.

A minute later, his need was again to see her face, and he again pulled back, but only to again kiss her, this time more deeply. 'My love,' he murmured, and as Delfi willingly returned his kiss he kissed her again. The next time he pulled back from her, a warm smile was about his mouth. 'I may not deserve you,' he told her, an emotional note there in his voice, 'but, by heavens, I'm going to keep you.'

'I'm glad about that,' Delfi laughed, in love with him, loved by him, and still not quite believing that this joy was hers.

'What contentment it is to hold you in my arms,' Boden breathed, and his smile suddenly broadening into a grin, 'I should have guessed what was in my heart when on that night in Chiang Mai market I caught hold of you when it looked as though you might fall, and discovered that— I liked having you in my arms.'

'That was before you knew?' Delfi queried in delight and when, still grinning, he nodded, 'I thought you were going to kiss me,' she confessed.

'I damn near did!' he growled, to her further delight.

'But—you thought better of it?'

'I realised I wasn't thinking at all and had better get my head together and get myself under control. Hell's bells, I was taking you into the hills for a month the next day!' His grin had faded, but his mouth was still curved upward as he said, 'I was still wondering what the blazes I was doing taking you with me the next morning. Yet—for some reason I hadn't faced— I felt unable to send you back to Bangkok.'

'You were—er—a bit snappy with me, as I recall,' Delfi murmured.

'Quite a masterly understatement!' Boden declared, and planted an adoring kiss on each side of her mouth. Then requested, 'Are you going to forgive me that what I didn't need while I was battling to keep that Land Rover on the road was for you to fall against me, for your fragrant hair to brush my face, and the warm gorgeous smell of you to play on my senses? Is it any wonder that, that night, when I was already far too much aware of you than I should be, I should later make a wrong decision?'

'Wrong decision?' she queried, loving him with all her heart, and still trying to take in that, incredibly, he loved her.

'What a short memory you have, Miss Washington,' he teased, and she fell in love with him some more. 'You'd gone to bed, then screamed, and I hared in to find you in mortal terror of a long-nosed whip-snake. What I *should* have done after I'd turfed it outside was to go back to my own quarters.'

'But what you did do,' she supplied, 'was come back to mine.'

'You were shaking so badly, I just couldn't leave you until you were calmer.' Tenderly, he kissed her. 'I didn't know then,' he breathed softly, 'that your fear was mostly on my account.'

'I never knew that real love was like that,' she replied.

'Your emotions for Renshaw weren't that strong?' he enquired, a hint of an edge coming to his tones.

'It wasn't real love that I felt for him,' Delfi swiftly answered, and was hugged with some fierceness for her trouble.

'The jealousy I've been through about him,' Boden confessed, but, as though deliberately turning his back on any other man in her life, 'You've no idea what you put me through that night—and ever since.'

'That night when Seri's pet snake, Preecha, chose to take up lodgings in my room?'

'The same,' Boden smiled. And looking down into her receptive violet eyes, 'Lord knows where I got the will-power from to leave you when Seri came calling his pet. But from somewhere I did—and then spent a night in mental trauma trying to get my head back together.'

'If it's any consolation, I had a fairly foul night myself,' Delfi confessed.

'As you once said to me—the very next day if I remember rightly when, with one thing and another, I'd had a pig of a day, losing my bearings and running out of road at one point—serves you right!' He grinned lovingly.

'Did my comment make you very angry?' she queried—a degree shamefacedly.

'Not a bit of it,' he revealed. 'You, and your spirit, amused me—which in turn made me realise that I was heartily glad to be back with you. Which feeling then put me back on the same tortuous treadmill I'd been on all through the wakeful hours of the previous night when, grabbing at what common sense I could find, I realised I was going to have to cool it.'

'Oh!' Delfi exclaimed as a sudden thought hit her. 'Was it really because I'd intimated that I wasn't too thrilled about jungles that you decided not to take me with you each day? Or...'

'Until that night, I'd every intention of taking you with me, my love,' Boden revealed gently. And, with his eyes adoring on her, 'Forgive me, sweetheart, but I was by then so aware of you that, what with the walls of our accommodation being so thin they might just as well have not been there, I felt it was too much of a risk to be with you—night *and* day.'

'Gracious!' she gasped, having had no idea at all of the inner torment he must have been going through. 'Was it really so nightmarish for you?'

He nodded, though smiled self-deprecatingly as he owned, 'Naturally, while part of me was of the view that I ought to get both of us out of there, part of me—the part that wanted your company exclusively—was insisting on reminding me that I'd promised my father that

I'd get him what information I could. From then on,' he cheerfully admitted, 'I seemed to be a constantly changing combination of contradictions.'

'In what way?' she couldn't resist asking.

'Where you were concerned, my dear,' he replied softly, 'I attempted to stay aloof, while at the same time was haunted by your face; beautiful, laughing, serious, lippy—I felt I knew all your expressions by heart. Against that, you were my secretary, and I'd never made a pass at any secretary in my employ in my life. So why should I be so disturbed—incensed even—when Seri let out that he'd posted a letter for you, and why should I immediately think you'd written to some man back in England?'

'You were jealous—even then?'

'Without admitting it for what it was, of course I was,' he agreed, confessing, 'Kevin Carroll, Renshaw, even Seri on one occasion I recall.'

'Seri!'

'He'd offered you a lift on his motorbike— I wasn't going to have you putting your arms around any man— or youth, for that matter!' Boden declared forcefully. Then suddenly, a wonderful, tender smile broke from him, and, 'And then one day— I discovered why.'

'The day— I took a ride on an elephant?' she guessed a trifle hesitantly, for all Boden was being totally open with her, still feeling a mite shy with him on the subject of their love.

'How adorable you are!' he breathed, for all the world as though he knew how she was feeling. Gently, he laid a feather-light kiss to her mouth. 'That was the day I felt restless and unable to settle and came back early,' he agreed. 'But you weren't there, and even while it was starting to sink in that life without you would be terrible, I hadn't then realised the depth of my feelings for you.'

'Oh,' Delfi sighed. 'Then you came looking for me.'

He shook his head. 'It was only that morning that we'd fired up at each other when I'd bloody-mindedly told you you weren't going anywhere on the back of any motorbike. So first I went to see if Seri's motorbike was standing where he usually parked it.'

'You thought I might have disobeyed you?'

'Are you saying you wouldn't have done if the mood was on you?'

Delfi laughed. 'You seem to know me very well, Mr McLaine!'

'I intend to know you better,' he assured her, and as she almost melted, 'Dearest Delfi, is it any wonder that I love you?' he asked, and tenderly kissed her, and kissed her again, and again. Then, eventually, he slowly pulled back to look worshippingly down into her lovely face. 'Where was I?' he asked.

Aware that her cheeks were more than a tinge pink, Delfi strove hard to remember. 'I—er—think you were just about to come looking for me,' she smiled.

'Ah, yes,' he murmured softly. 'I came looking for you and saw this woman who cared not at all for the jungle—lo and behold—atop of an elephant, would you believe, come from out of nowhere else. I knew myself deeply in love with you when, joy in my thumping heart, I held you close in my arms for several most wonderful moments.'

'Oh, darling!' Delfi murmured the endearment shyly. 'It was pure heaven for me to be in your arms, but I soon began to be afraid that, if I didn't let go of you, you'd be bound to get some idea of how much I cared for you.'

'If only I'd known, I'd have saved myself a whole load of grief, when later that same night what started out as harmonious conversation degenerated when the green-eyed monster again got to me.'

'When you asked me why I'd left England,' Delfi catalogued.

'I should have left it alone and just enjoyed the pleasure of your company, but I couldn't,' he admitted. 'I was pushed and pushed by that demon jealousy that wouldn't let me alone.'

'And consequently,' Delfi took up bravely, 'you were totally disgusted with me when I told you that Hugh Renshaw was engaged to my sister.'

'I was never disgusted with you!' he at once denied. And while Delfi stared at him with ever-widening eyes, 'Ye gods, my sweet love,' he said forcefully, 'I was never, *ever* disgusted with you.'

'You weren't?' She found it difficult to believe.

That was until, 'What I was,' he told her forthrightly, 'was scared as hell at the violence of my jealous feelings to hear you confirm that you were in love with another man. I had to get away from the building, from you. My darling, I had that day come face to face with the truth of what my feelings were for you. I just could not take it that you were in love with somebody else. I needed to get away until I'd got my self-control back together.'

'Oh, my love,' Delfi crooned, and, because she couldn't help it, she leaned forward and kissed him.

'You can do that again any time,' Boden gently invited, but when she smiled he resumed, 'After that night, of course, even though jealousy was forever rife within me, I determined to keep my distance. That was—until last Saturday when I didn't see you at all in the morning before I went off.'

'You were later than usual coming back that night,' Delfi remembered without any trouble, and, growing more confident in his love, confessed, 'I was on the point of going to ask Seri to take me on his bike to look for you—when I first of all saw the lights of the Land Rover, then——'

His exclamation of, 'You were that worried about me!' caused her to break off. Then both his hands were cupping her face. 'So, you really *do* love me!' he breathed.

'Didn't you believe me?'

'Yes—but—— Oh, come here,' he cried, and she was close up against his heart once more, and he was pouring endearments down about her and telling her how he had deliberately stayed away that night, but then, having delayed his return to the camp, he had been beset by such a desperate need to see her that he had driven back so fast it was a wonder, on such non-roads, that he'd arrived back in one piece. 'Can you imagine my disappointment,' he went on, 'that, having very nearly broken my neck to get back to you, I should then disappointingly find that you had already eaten and gone to bed?'

'I'm sorry,' she at once apologised.

'I should think you are!' he smiled. 'Though, even while I'm wondering what I'd expected but that you wouldn't wait up for me, I donned my determined-not-to-seek-you-out hat. I went to bed in a most beleaguered frame of mind.'

'If it's any consolation, I wasn't having a very happy time of it either,' she confessed. 'That is, I just couldn't sleep—not until in the early hours, when I sneezed, and you called out, "Bless you!"'

'How I remember that!' Boden took over. 'Suddenly, we'd communicated, and it was as if some black cloud that had been hanging over me was lifted.'

'For you too?' Smilingly, he nodded, and Delfi went on to remind him, 'The very next morning you asked me if I'd like to come with you.'

'I'd at last accepted the inevitable,' he cheerfully owned. 'I wanted you with me all the time. To that end, I had the quickest shower on record that night, in order to get to our mutual sitting-room the faster.'

'I didn't know...!' she started to gasp, but, feeling suddenly rapturously happy that Boden felt so much for her, she could not go on.

'What is it?' he asked urgently, and finding his own reason for her choked look. 'Are you remembering the swine I turned into before that night was through?'

'I wasn't actually,' Delfi quickly assured him, 'I was just a bit—er—full, that you—um—care for me so much.'

'I love you with all of my heart,' he breathed tenderly, and kissed her gently, and for a long time.

Stars were shining in Delfi's eyes when he at last pulled back from her. 'Darling Boden,' she whispered, and for many long moments they just sat and stared at each other in wonder at their shared love. Then Delfi had to tell him, 'I'm sorry I ran away from you.'

'Sweet love, after the brute I was to you that last evening, you were fully justified. Knowing your pride, your spirit, it didn't take me long to realise that I'd given you very little option.' He shook his head as though to clear it of the grim memory of finding her gone, then recalled, 'You'd said, that last evening, that you were going to turn in—but I didn't want you to go then either. But in my haste to tell you "Don't go" we somehow bumped into each other and, while my heart was thundering so loud I thought you might hear it, we were suddenly in each other's arms.'

'I was totally lost to everything,' Delfi admitted dreamily. 'That is,' she all at once remembered, 'until you demanded to know whether I was still in love with Hugh.'

'Excuse my jealous heart, sweet love, that even in the bliss of your embrace that canker jealousy should still find space to eat away at me,' Boden apologised.

'Forgive me too,' she said quietly, 'that—in covering up my love for you— I should provoke you so. I didn't know, then, that you loved me.'

'How could you know? With the two of us so proud, so sensitive on the subject, we were both trying to hide it.'

'I'm sorry,' she apologised prettily.

'So, too, am I,' he smiled, and kissed her.

'It was the last time I saw you in Thailand,' Delfi commented some seconds later.

'Don't remind me!' Boden exclaimed. 'Lord knows how, wanting you like crazy as I did, I found the strength to spurn you. I was green-eyed-monster-assisted, of course, but, if it's any salve, my love, I didn't dare come back to the building that night.'

'Where did you go?'

'Heaven alone knows! I desperately wanted you, I knew that, but as dawn appeared I still wasn't risking coming anywhere near you.'

'Good—lord!' Delfi gasped. 'You thought—should we speak to each other—perhaps strike sparks off each other—that we might again somehow find ourselves in each other's arms?'

'Something like that,' he owned.

'Which is why, without setting foot inside the building again, you took off in the Land Rover.'

'To return—to find you gone.'

'I thought—that you were so disgusted at my behaviour, so contemptuous of what you thought were my standards—in using you for a substitute lover—that you'd decided not to put up with seeing me more than you had to.'

'Never that!' he exclaimed, and holding her fiercely to him, 'My stars, have you any idea of how utterly devastated I was when I found you gone?'

'You discovered that Seri had given me a lift to Chiang Rai airport?'

'In no time flat!' he replied. 'And also that you were making for England.' While she rather gained an impression that poor Seri had been put through quite a third degree, Boden continued, 'I then spent a sleepless night deciding that if you loved Renshaw so badly that you'd risk your sister's happiness by returning to England—which, since he was the reason you left must mean that by returning you intended to take him from her—then I could stand no chance.'

'You honestly thought that?' Delfi asked in astonishment. 'That I'd gone to Hugh?'

'My usually clear-thinking brain had seized up where you were concerned,' he replied with a smile. 'By then I was totally fed up with everything. Certainly fed up with a holiday that wasn't a holiday and which I'd only agreed on because my father, in one of his "It's time I spent some time with my own son" moments, had suggested—and which I in a moment of being jaded with more normal holiday pursuits agreed to.' Delfi loved it that Boden was sharing his personal thoughts with her.

'It hasn't been much of a holiday, has it?' she sympathised.

'I should have known better,' he agreed with a grin, explaining, 'I seem to have spent a good part of my life doing "things" for my father.' He shrugged. 'Other than being occasionally irritated, it's never particularly bothered me that in my relationship with him I was the one who usually ended up holding the short straw. It's odd, I suppose,' he went on, 'that while in the cut and thrust of business one gives no quarter, yet when it comes to families—one stands such a lot.'

'You love your father,' Delfi stated softly.

'As you love your sister,' Boden replied, and with his eyes firm on hers, tender on hers, 'Loving my father as I do, you loving your sister as you do, I could quite appreciate how you would feel so guilty about loving her fiancé that you would make the decision you did, to leave England. But not until yesterday when, after another tormented night, I got out of bed did I realise that what I could *not* see was how, loving your sister so strongly, you could return to England to ruin her happiness.'

'Ah,' Delfi murmured.

'Ah, indeed, minx,' he murmured adoringly. 'I then had to ask myself—was it on account of Renshaw that you were returning anyhow? The next question, my dear, followed automatically. Could you, loving him the way you had tried to make me believe you did, be the inflamed and passionate way you'd been with me—even if you had been using me as a substitute? From what I knew of you, dearest Delfi— I thought not. Could it be, then, that by your leaving me you felt that *I* was a greater threat than Renshaw? Could it be— I hardly dared think it—that you did not love him, but loved—*me*?'

'You decided to come and find out?'

'I caught the very first plane I could.'

'Oh, Boden,' she sighed.

He kissed the tip of her lovely nose, and then told her, 'I landed on your doorstep and took heart, on introducing myself to your mother as someone you'd met in

Thailand, that she seemed quite pleased to invite me in.
Then very nearly lost all hope when, while we were
waiting for you, she passed the time away by telling me
that your sister was due to marry someone called
Lawrence.'

'You thought that I might be engaged to Hugh?'

'I wanted to leave then and there, then found that—
I just couldn't!'

'I'm glad you stayed,' Delfi whispered.

'So am I!' he ardently declared. Then, somewhat ob-
scurely, she thought, demanded quite urgently, 'We don't
have to wait for your sister to be married first, do we?'

'First?' she queried.

'What did you think I meant when I told you that I
was going to keep you?' he enquired, and not waiting
for her reply, 'I'm going to marry you,' he told her, 'and
soon.'

'But—but . . .' Flabbergasted, Delfi found that she
couldn't so much as string a sentence together.

'For heaven's sake!' burst aggressively from him as
he misunderstood her hesitation. 'You're not turning me
down *now*!'

'No—no!' Delfi hurriedly found her voice to assure
him. 'It was just that— I didn't think... Well, you stated,
quite categorically, ages ago, that with your father's
record before you—his being married three times—you'd
decided that marriage was something you could do
without.'

'It's true, I always have felt that my father's penchant
for marrying seemed an excellent reason to avoid——'

'You told Dr Phothiat that marriage was not a step
you'd ever contemplated,' Delfi, her heart in the wildest
flutter, reminded him.

'And I, as I looked at you, suddenly experienced a
most peculiar, never-before-felt sensation—and realised

that I seemed to be losing my aversion to the thought of being married.'

'You're—sure?'

'I'm sure I'll go mad if you don't give me the straight "yes" I'm beginning to panic about!' he stated bluntly. 'Are you going to marry me, Delfi?' he demanded.

'Yes,' she accepted promptly—and the next she knew she was tight up against his heart.

'My love, my love,' he breathed. Then he kissed her long and lingeringly, and when, finally, he drew back to look into her shining violet eyes, 'I confess, I've been hit so hard that I've barely known where I am half of my time,' he told her hoarsely.

'Oh, my dear,' she whispered huskily.

'Truly, my love, I need you,' he murmured.

HARLEQUIN
Romance®

Coming Next Month

BIG SUMMER READ

Summer Reading At Its Best

In July, Harlequin and Silhouette bring readers the Big Summer Read Program. Heat up your summer with these four exciting new novels by top Harlequin and Silhouette authors.

SOMEWHERE IN TIME by Barbara Bretton
YESTERDAY COMES TOMORROW by Rebecca Flanders
A DAY IN APRIL by Mary Lynn Baxter
LOVE CHILD by Patricia Coughlin

From time travel to fame and fortune, this program offers something for everyone.

Available at your favorite retail outlet.

BSR

"GET AWAY FROM IT ALL" SWEEPSTAKES

HERE'S HOW THE SWEEPSTAKES WORKS

NO PURCHASE NECESSARY

To enter each drawing, complete the appropriate Official Entry Form or a 3" by 5" index card by hand-printing your name, address and phone number and the trip destination that the entry is being submitted for (i.e., Caneel Bay, Canyon Ranch or London and the English Countryside) and mailing it to: Get Away From It All Sweepstakes, P.O. Box 1397, Buffalo, New York 14269-1397.

No responsibility is assumed for lost, late or misdirected mail. Entries must be sent separately with first class postage affixed, and be received by: 4/15/92 for the Caneel Bay Vacation Drawing, 5/15/92 for the Canyon Ranch Vacation Drawing and 6/15/92 for the London and the English Countryside Vacation Drawing. Sweepstakes is open to residents of the U.S. (except Puerto Rico) and Canada, 21 years of age or older as of 5/31/92.

For complete rules send a self-addressed, stamped (WA residents need not affix return postage) envelope to: Get Away From It All Sweepstakes, P.O. Box 4892, Blair, NE 68009.

© 1992 HARLEQUIN ENTERPRISES LTD.   SWP-RLS

- -

"GET AWAY FROM IT ALL" SWEEPSTAKES

HERE'S HOW THE SWEEPSTAKES WORKS

NO PURCHASE NECESSARY

To enter each drawing, complete the appropriate Official Entry Form or a 3" by 5" index card by hand-printing your name, address and phone number and the trip destination that the entry is being submitted for (i.e., Caneel Bay, Canyon Ranch or London and the English Countryside) and mailing it to: Get Away From It All Sweepstakes, P.O. Box 1397, Buffalo, New York 14269-1397.

No responsibility is assumed for lost, late or misdirected mail. Entries must be sent separately with first class postage affixed, and be received by: 4/15/92 for the Caneel Bay Vacation Drawing, 5/15/92 for the Canyon Ranch Vacation Drawing and 6/15/92 for the London and the English Countryside Vacation Drawing. Sweepstakes is open to residents of the U.S. (except Puerto Rico) and Canada, 21 years of age or older as of 5/31/92.

For complete rules send a self-addressed, stamped (WA residents need not affix return postage) envelope to: Get Away From It All Sweepstakes, P.O. Box 4892, Blair, NE 68009.

© 1992 HARLEQUIN ENTERPRISES LTD.   SWP-RLS

"GET AWAY FROM IT ALL"

Brand-new Subscribers-Only Sweepstakes

OFFICIAL ENTRY FORM

This entry must be received by: May 15, 1992
This month's winner will be notified by: May 31, 1992
Trip must be taken between: June 30, 1992—June 30, 1993

YES, I want to win the Canyon Ranch vacation for two. I
understand the prize includes round-trip airfare and the two
additional prizes revealed in the BONUS PRIZES insert.

Name _____

Address _____

City _____

State/Prov._____ Zip/Postal Code _____

Daytime phone number _____
                                        (Area Code)

Return entries with invoice in envelope provided. Each book in this shipment has two
entry coupons — and the more coupons you enter, the better your chances of winning!
© 1992 HARLEQUIN ENTERPRISES LTD.   2M-CPN

"GET AWAY FROM IT ALL"

Brand-new Subscribers-Only Sweepstakes

OFFICIAL ENTRY FORM

This entry must be received by: May 15, 1992
This month's winner will be notified by: May 31, 1992
Trip must be taken between: June 30, 1992—June 30, 1993

YES, I want to win the Canyon Ranch vacation for two. I
understand the prize includes round-trip airfare and the two
additional prizes revealed in the BONUS PRIZES insert.

Name _____

Address _____

City _____

State/Prov._____ Zip/Postal Code _____

Daytime phone number _____
                                        (Area Code)

Return entries with invoice in envelope provided. Each book in this shipment has two
entry coupons — and the more coupons you enter, the better your chances of winning!
© 1992 HARLEQUIN ENTERPRISES LTD.   2M-CPN